A Dance To Remember

A Dance To Remember
© 2004 by Melanie L. Wilber
Revised and updated, 2022
All Rights Reserved

Dedication

For My Jesus
You lead, I'll follow

Go out into the world uncorrupted, a breath of fresh air in this society. Provide people with a glimpse of good living and of the living God.

Philippians 2:15
(THE MESSAGE)

Chapter One

"Okay, I think I'm ready," Amber said, securing the clasp on her necklace and glancing herself over in the bathroom mirror one last time.

"You look fabulous," Kerri replied, giving her a sincere smile. She had been helping her get ready for the Winter Dance taking place tonight.

"Thanks, Kerri," she said, giving her a hug.

"Thank you, Amber," she replied, holding her tightly.

"For what?"

Kerri released her and spoke seriously, appearing as though she might cry. "For loving my brother the way you do. He's very special, and I always want the best for him."

Kerri smiled and managed to keep the tears from spilling over. Amber wasn't as successful. Kerri grabbed a tissue and dabbed the wetness under her eyes. Amber took a deep breath and gave her a little smile, thankful for her words. She didn't always believe in her value to Seth, and his family, so she appreciated the reminder.

Seth had come to her house this morning. They had lunch with her parents and took a quiet walk at the lake before coming here to his house so she could get into her dress and everything. She was hoping for a romantic evening—a dance to remember like her grandparents had shared all those years ago. She had written their story for her *Creative Writing* assignment earlier this week and turned it in yesterday, feeling really good about the way it had turned out, and a bit surprised. She had taken the class to learn how to write better, and she had learned many useful skills, but mostly she felt she had discovered a talent in herself she didn't know she possessed.

Her current thoughts, however, were not on school or anything else except having a great time with Seth tonight. Last spring they had gone to Prom together, and she'd had a nice time, but she had also been pretty nervous because it had been her first formal dance. She didn't feel nervous about tonight, just excited. She was looking forward to being with Seth, letting him treat her special, and dancing with him.

"I'll go see if Seth is ready," Kerri said, stepping out of the bathroom. "And he better not have changed his hair."

Amber laughed and was already glad they had decided to go to Seth's school dance rather than her own if for no other reason than the past hour she'd had with Kerri. His twin sister treated Seth differently than anyone else. Only Kerri could get him to change his hairstyle. Only Kerri could talk him into wearing new clothes he didn't think were his style but she assured him were perfect. And only Kerri could have made the past hour so much fun. She had a lot of great stories to tell about her brother, some from when they were young and others from last week.

Amber turned off the bathroom light and walked into the connecting master bedroom Seth's parents shared. His mom had several photographs placed around the room, and Amber stepped over to one of the large dressers to look at the picture of Seth's parents that had been taken on their wedding day.

They looked incredibly young, but it was definitely them. His mom looked a lot like Kerri did now, and his dad resembled Seth somewhat, although there were definite differences. Seth's dad was very tall with broad shoulders, but his mother was petite, at least a foot shorter than her husband. Seth seemed to have inherited a good mix of traits from them, having similar facial features as his dad but a smaller and shorter stature like his mom. He'd grown a few inches over the summer, but unless he had another growth spurt, he wasn't likely to make it to six feet. Right now he was about five-ten, and Amber thought he was the perfect height. Slightly taller than herself, but not so much she had to strain her neck every time she kissed him.

Feeling her nerves kick in a bit, Amber took a deep breath and couldn't wait to see Seth. There were times she felt perfectly content to be with him in a group setting. Sharing his presence with family and friends had its place, and she knew it was wise for them to not spend too much time completely alone together, but there were times when having him all to herself was exactly what she wanted, and she felt that way tonight.

Seth had called her on Thursday with a slight change of plans she hoped wouldn't interfere with that too much. Originally his dad was going to be their chauffeur tonight like her dad had been for them last spring when they'd gone to the prom. But then Seth had talked to one of his good friends Amber had met when she'd gone on activities with Seth's youth group, and Matt and his girlfriend along with two other couples had decided to rent a limo together, and they were looking for one more couple to go with them.

When Seth had asked her about it, she said she didn't mind riding with the others to and from the dance but she would prefer to have dinner with him alone. He said he wanted that too, and so his dad was driving them to the downtown restaurant but then the limo would be picking them up to take them to the dance and to wherever the group decided to go afterwards.

Seth would have declined Matt's offer and gone with their original plans to have a more private time for just the two of them, but he was concerned about Matt and his girlfriend and what they might decide to do after the dance. Apparently Matt had recently gotten back together with the girl he had dated last spring and part of the summer, and Seth wasn't too sure they had the healthiest relationship. He didn't want to see his friend make a stupid mistake on a night like this that could easily take a bad turn if Matt didn't have the right kind of friends watching out for him, and Seth didn't have too much confidence in the others that were going along.

But at least they would have a nice dinner together and get to ride in a limo—something she had never done before. Feeling the need to pray for herself and Seth, along with Matt and his other friends, Amber did so and then she heard a soft knock on the closed bedroom door.

Crossing the room, she opened the door and saw what she expected: Seth standing there appearing incredibly handsome in his nice tuxedo and a new hairstyle she knew he probably wasn't too sure about but she thought looked great. Kerri had spiked the short brown strands on top of his head in a classy-looking way, but Seth had always gone with more conservative styles in the past, even on special occasions.

She had almost forgotten about her own appearance until she saw the look on Seth's face. Although he had seen her in a nice dress with her hair and face done up for Prom last spring, she had managed to have a different look this time. Her dress was a completely different style, and the deeper shade of fabric made her look elegant, she thought, and instead of having her hair up, Kerri had straightened it along with doing her makeup. She had been surprised at the results but pretended not to notice his wonderfully sweet expression and put on her shy-girl face.

"Hi. Are you my date for tonight?"

He smiled. "Yes, I believe I am."

"Wow. You're dreamy. What's your name?"

"Seth," he played along. "And you are?"

"Amber."

He stepped forward and kissed her on the cheek. "It's very nice to meet you, Amber. Do you mind if I call you sweetheart?"

She laughed. "I'd like that."

He placed his hands around her waist and pulled her close to him. "You look beautiful."

"Thank you."

"Do you mind if I change one thing?"

"What?"

He slipped his hand inside his jacket and pulled out a necklace from the inner pocket. It had a beautiful heart-shaped pendant with little diamond-like stones all around the edge. She recognized it as one she had pointed out to him when they had gone shopping over Thanksgiving Weekend and he was looking for Christmas gift ideas.

"I was going to save this for Christmas, but I thought you might like to wear it tonight," he said.

She smiled and removed the necklace she had put on, the one he had given her last year shortly after they started dating. The simple heart on the delicate chain was special to her, but this new one was really nice, and she was glad he had decided to give it to her now because it wasn't something she would likely wear every day but only on special occasions.

After putting the new one around her neck, he kissed her and said they should probably get going. They went downstairs, posed for pictures in front of the fireplace in the formal living room, and then went out to get into the back seat of the roomy family sedan.

On the way to the restaurant and all through dinner, Seth seemed his normal self, and she felt relaxed and happy. She loved times like this with him. Times where they could talk about serious things, plans for the future, what God had been teaching them both lately, and little things she knew were just between the two of them, not something Seth would be sharing with his family or other friends.

When they both finished eating, it wasn't time for the limo to arrive, but they decided to go out to the lobby of the nice restaurant and wait anyway. Amber began to sense some nervousness on Seth's part. He spoke less and had a look on his face she had grown to know well. He had serious thoughts going through his mind, and she knew they likely had to do with his friends and what the rest of this evening would hold.

She began to have uneasy feelings also. She remembered Hope telling her about experiences during and after dances she'd been to. Hope had lost her virginity after her first formal dance her sophomore year, and another time she had gotten very drunk and didn't remember what had happened at the after-prom party she went to.

Amber didn't know Seth's friends well enough to speculate if anything that serious might be the fate of some of them tonight, but Seth didn't usually worry about his friends and keep a watchful eye on them unless he had a legitimate reason. He had an amazing ability to read people. He knew when someone wasn't being honest with him or when there was more going on in a situation than could be seen on the surface.

"Do you want to go outside and pray?" she asked. He hadn't voiced any of his concerns, but she could see them written all over his face.

He sighed. "Yeah, let's go," he said, leading her outside into the chilly winter air. He removed his jacket and wrapped it around her shoulders. They walked down the street to a storefront that was closed this time of night. Seth took her hands and prayed about the remainder of their evening and especially for Matt.

He admitted his feelings of inadequacy to Jesus freely, not wanting to make judgments about his friend, but not wanting to turn the other way and let him make a stupid mistake tonight either. He also shared his longing for this to be a special night for the two of them but knowing that might be difficult for them to do. He didn't look or sound much better after he had finished praying, making Amber more aware this night had the potential to turn out differently than she could even imagine.

"Maybe we shouldn't go with them," he said. "I could call my dad and have him drive us to the dance."

Amber thought seriously about his suggestion. Maybe this wasn't something they should get involved in. Maybe Seth was trying to take concerns on himself he couldn't do anything about anyway. Maybe it wasn't their place to interfere with whatever his friends decided to do or not do.

But she didn't think Seth could put it out of his mind at this point. If he couldn't do anything to keep his friends from making bad choices, so be it, but if he could and didn't try, she knew he would carry the burden on his shoulders if anything happened and he heard about it later.

"You know, Seth," she said, squeezing his fingers gently. "Our relationship is about a lot more than going to the movies and to dances and having a good time together. It's about our lives, and the lives of our friends, and reasons God has brought us together we may not know about yet."

"Do you think this might be one of those times?"

"Yes, I do. Maybe we can't change anything that happens tonight, but maybe we can. God has used us to make a difference for those around us before, why not tonight? Maybe Matt is counting on you being around. He knows the strong stand you take. Maybe that's why he asked you to come, even if he would never admit that."

Seth took her into his arms and held her close. Her own anxiety melted away. If she had Seth by her side tonight, she knew she could make it through any situation they faced.

"Since Jesus already answered one of my prayers," Seth said, "I suppose I can count on Him to answer the rest."

"What prayer was that?"

"I asked Him to give me strength and peace, and He just did that—through you."

She smiled. "That's my God."

"Will you stand by me no matter what happens tonight, Amber?"

"Absolutely."

He started to kiss her but then stopped, spotting something beyond her. She turned and saw the limo coming up the street toward them. He took her hand and led them to the car as it pulled along the curb in front of the restaurant. The back door opened, and Matt got out. He seemed excited to see them and teased Seth about his hair.

"Who talked you into that? Your beautiful girlfriend, or your sister?"

"Shut up, man," Seth laughed, stepping to the side and letting her get into the car ahead of him.

Amber lowered herself onto the seat and moved over to allow Seth to sit beside her. Matt got in first and took his seat beside the girl she knew must be his girlfriend, and then Seth got in behind him.

By the time the limo had pulled onto the street and Seth had introduced her to everyone, Amber had detected the distinct smell of alcohol permeating the air.

Chapter Two

On the ten-minute drive to the hotel where the dance was being held, Amber remained quiet and knew she had entered a different world than the one she and Seth had been in all day. It seemed unreal. She had been around Matt several times in the past, and he had always been pleasant and friendly. But it didn't take long to figure out he had been drinking. He was acting like himself, but not really. He laughed too much at things that weren't very funny. He kissed his girlfriend a bit too heavily right in front of everyone.

And Clarissa, his girlfriend, was also acting too giddy. She was wearing a very tight, very skimpy dress that made Amber want to put a blindfold over Seth's eyes. Amber didn't think she had met the others in the car before, so she didn't know if they were acting more like their normal selves or not. One of the girls, Erin, had on a beautiful, tasteful dress but didn't appear to be having too great of a time.

When they arrived at the hotel, they all got out of the limo, and Amber saw Seth hang back and pull Matt aside. She walked into the lobby with the others, including Clarissa, and then followed the other girls to the bathroom.

"I love your dress," she said to Erin.

"Thanks," she said, giving her a tiny smile. It was the first time she had seen her smile or heard her speak.

"Did you have a nice dinner?"

"Yeah, it was nice," she said, not sounding too convincing.

"How long have you and Pete been dating?"

"Oh, this is the first time we've been out," she said.

"Are you both seniors?"

"Pete's a senior. I'm a sophomore."

Amber didn't have to ask Erin any more questions to know she needed to watch out for her tonight, and Seth confirmed that later when they were dancing to a slow song. He had stayed outside, talking to Matt for ten minutes before they both came inside.

"I'm glad we decided to come with them if for no other reason than to watch out for Erin," Seth said. "She has no idea what she's gotten herself into with Pete. I'm definitely not letting him out of my sight tonight."

"How did your talk with Matt go?"

"Okay. He said he only had a few sips of a hard lemonade Clarissa brought and they shared between the restaurant and meeting us. I told him to think before he does anything tonight, and he said, 'Yes, Dad.'"

"You're doing the right thing," she encouraged him. "He might not appreciate it tonight, but he'll thank you later."

He sighed and pulled her closer to him. "I'm sorry, Amber. This isn't how tonight was supposed to go. It was supposed to be about you and me."

She lifted her eyes and smiled at him. "It is about you and me. You and me making a difference together."

For the next hour everything went smoothly, and Amber got in several nice dances with Seth. She was surprised when Matt asked her to dance. Clarissa was dancing with someone else at the time, and Seth had asked Erin while Pete was off dancing with other girls and had pretty much abandoned her for twenty minutes.

Matt was a perfect gentleman with her, and she enjoyed having the chance to talk to him and see him for the way he really was, instead of the way he'd been acting most of the night. After a minute of small-talk, she dared to say what she thought he may need to be reminded of.

"Seth thinks of you as one of his best friends, Matt. You know that, right?"

He appeared surprised at her bluntness, and he sighed. "Yes, I know that."

She expected him to comment on Seth's overly concerned behavior tonight, but instead he said something else.

"And Seth is completely in love with you. You know that, right?"

She smiled. "That's what he tells me."

"I know it's true," he said. "He's always been a good guy. Solid. Happy. Well-liked. But since he's been with you, he's been all of that and more. Last year I thought it was a phase; his first girlfriend—the newness would wear off and he'd come down and live with the rest of us again. But he's so far gone on you—four years of being his friend, and I've never seen him like this."

She smiled. "I think he's pretty great too. And there are days I still can't believe he picked me."

"You know what he said after he met you at Taco Bell?"

"You were there?"

"Yes, and I'd never seen him like that before. After he decided to go talk to you, we were laughing because you had spilled your Pepsi all over him, and he said, "I was right, she's going to camp. Now I have a whole week to convince her she should be with me."

Amber laughed. Kerri had told her something else related to that week she hadn't known until tonight. Kerri hadn't known anything about Seth having his eye on her until Saturday morning on the ride home. He sat beside her in the van and showed her the bracelet he bought and told Kerri what he liked about her and why he felt God had intended for them to meet.

"He said, 'If the camp didn't have the rule about no kissing, I would have kissed her out on that canoe.'" And then Kerri said, "I knew he was serious at that point because Seth had always been very adamant about not kissing a girl until he knew for sure it was right."

When the dance with Matt ended, Amber walked back to where they had been sitting, met Seth there, and asked him if they could go outside for a few minutes. He agreed and they went out a side door that led to a courtyard area. Once they were somewhat alone, she smiled at him and asked him to kiss her.

Several times while they had been dancing, Amber had seen couples surrounding them who were practically making-out right there on the dance floor, or guys who had their hands in places they shouldn't be. She had closed her eyes each time and cherished the feeling of being held in Seth's arms in an affectionate but non-sexual way. A way that made her feel loved and treasured, but not lusted after.

As Seth kissed her gently and passionately now, she had that exact same feeling, and it made her cry.

"What's wrong, sweetheart?" Seth asked in such a caring way, it made her cry more. He held her close to him and waited for her to stop. When she did, she explained her tears and the sudden need she had to have a few minutes alone with him.

"I love that we could be here at the dance, all alone somewhere, or in my living room with my family, and you would treat me the exact same way. I love that from the beginning I've been able to trust you and I've never had to be anyone but myself, and that's the girl you wanted."

He didn't say anything. He smiled and kissed her again and then held her close to him and started dancing to the soft music being played through the courtyard speakers.

"I love you, Amber. And you're the only one for me."

After they were back inside and had been sitting with the fourth couple in their group who seemed to be having a nice time together, Seth voiced his concern that he hadn't seen Matt and Clarissa for awhile and went looking for them, and she went to get something to drink. When she returned to the table, Pete and Erin were there, and Erin looked positively miserable. She had seen them dancing together during the previous song, and Pete had been holding Erin very close to him and kissing her way too much for their first date, in her opinion. And if the look on Erin's face was any indication, she thought so too.

"I need to go to the bathroom," Amber whispered in her ear after she finished her punch. "Want to go with me?"

Erin agreed and once they were in the confines of the ladies' room that was mostly deserted at the moment, Amber asked her if she was okay.

"No," Erin said, appearing close to tears. "Pete's always seemed so nice at church, but here he's completely different. He keeps trying to kiss me, and I don't even know him. It's grossing me out!"

"Do you want to go home?"

"Yes, but I don't think that's possible."

"Call your mom and dad and have them come pick you up."

Erin shook her head. "I spent so much money on this dress. If I call my mom and go home early, she will have a fit!"

"So let her have a fit. At least you won't end up wasting any more kisses on Pete. You deserve better, Erin."

Tears overflowed Erin's beautiful green eyes. She took out her phone but couldn't bring herself to call home. Amber asked her if she had any older siblings or friends who could come get her. Erin shook her head and really started crying at that point.

Amber used her own phone and called Kerri. Amber told her what was going on and asked if she could drive over and pick up Erin. Kerri agreed without hesitation. Amber left Erin in the bathroom and went back to the ballroom to find Seth, who had apparently found Clarissa and Matt and was sitting at the table with them and the others.

"I need to talk to you," she whispered in his ear.

He got out of his chair and followed her into the hallway. After she told him what she had done, he smiled and gave her a loving embrace. "I love you, Amber."

Seth said he would tell Pete that Erin wasn't feeling well, and Amber went back to sit with her in the bathroom until Kerri arrived fifteen minutes later. While they waited, Erin asked why she was doing this for her, and Amber told her about Hope.

"I'd hate to see something like that happen to you. There are good guys out there. I found one, and you can too. Pray for him and then wait for him—for as long as it takes. I promise it will be worth it."

"Is Seth really as nice as he seems?" Erin asked.

"Yes, he is. He asked permission before he kissed me the first time, and we've been dating for over a year and he's never touched me—you know what I mean by that—not even once. Wait for a guy like that, okay?"

"Okay. Thanks, Amber," she said, accepting her warm hug as Kerri entered the lounge area where they had been waiting. Erin seemed embarrassed when Amber introduced them, but Kerri quickly set her at ease.

"I've been there, sweetie," she said.

"And now she's waiting for the right one," Amber said.

"Yep. I know he's out there somewhere."

When the three of them walked out to the lobby, Pete was waiting by the doors along with Seth. Pete stepped forward to talk to Erin, sounding very sweet and concerned in that moment, offering to call a taxi and see her home himself, but Erin wasn't buying it.

"I'm not sick, Pete. I'm not having a good time. I'd rather have Kerri take me home."

Erin left with Kerri, and Amber remained behind with Seth. Pete had a confused look on his face for a moment, then glanced at her and back to Seth.

"You can't treat girls like that, Pete."

"You should mind your own business, Kirkwood."

Amber thought Pete might hit him, but Seth appeared fearless.

"Erin is my sister in Christ, and you are my brother. That makes both of you my business."

Pete shoved him in the chest and stepped past him, mumbled something under his breath, and walked out the front doors without looking back. Once he was gone, Amber stepped over and wrapped her arms around Seth's neck. He held her in return. He was trembling.

"You're my hero," she said.

He laughed. "Let's go before he comes back."

They returned to the ballroom, heard a slow dance beginning, and enjoyed the next few minutes. Seth held her close, and neither of them spoke until the end of the song when Seth informed her of some news he had learned while she'd been in the bathroom with Erin.

"They're planning on going to a party after the dance. Supposedly it's a clean one, but I'll believe that when I see it."

"Does that mean we're going too?"

"For awhile at least," he said. "If it's legitimate, then I'll have my dad come pick us up there, but if it's not, I don't know. I'm just playing this by ear."

Clarissa and Matt ended up dancing most of the time for the last half-hour. The other couple, Tawnya and Shane, seemed to be having a genuinely good time, but they were both feeling tired and sat with them at the table. Shane was a junior and knew Matt through playing soccer. He had transferred to Lincoln from Portland Christian this year, and he and Tawnya had been dating since this summer.

They both went to a smaller church together on the east side but had been going to Sunday night youth group at Emmanuel the last few months. Their church only had a midweek youth night they couldn't usually attend because of sports. Tawnya played volleyball and basketball, and they talked about their mutual interests.

"What happened to Pete? Did he take Erin home?" Shane asked.

Seth went ahead and told them the truth of the matter and then he also let them in on something about this party they were all going to.

"I don't want to tell you what to do," Seth said, "but I've been to one of the parties this guy's had before—and heard about some others—and even though it's supposed to be alcohol-free and all that, I'll be very surprised if it is. They have a great indoor pool and two hot tubs, one by the pool and another one in a more out-of-the-way place, should I say? Anyway, the only reason we're going is because I need to keep an eye on Matt, and if you don't think a party like that is where you want to be, you might want to say so."

Shane looked at Tawnya. "I'd rather go out for dessert."

"Yeah, me too," Tawnya said.

When the final song was announced, the four of them went out to dance one last time and then met up with Clarissa and Matt outside before finding their limo and getting in. Matt wanted to know if Pete had taken a cab or what. Seth said he didn't know. Matt decided to call him to make sure they weren't leaving him behind.

"He's at the party already," Matt informed them after he hung up. "He wanted to know if you were coming."

"Me?" Seth asked.

"Yes. Why did he want to know that?"

"Probably because he hopes I'm not."

"Why? What did you do?"

"It doesn't matter," he said and changed the subject. "How about if we go out for dessert and skip the party?"

"Seth, don't start," Matt said.

"Start what?"

"You know what."

"Matt, Jake's parties aren't that great, and you know it. I don't think that's where any of us should be tonight."

"If you don't want to have a beer, then don't have one."

"It's not about the beer, Matt. It's about the atmosphere. It's about taking a stand and not being there because you know it's not right."

"We're just going to use the pool," Matt argued.

"Uh-huh, and what have you seen the girls wearing at Jake's pool parties?"

Matt didn't answer this time. Clarissa glared at Seth.

"What's that supposed to mean?"

"You know what it means, Clarissa."

"It's a pool party! What do you expect the girls to wear?"

"Something that covers more than their underwear would."

Clarissa didn't respond to that and faked a headache instead, laying her head on Matt's shoulder and pressing on her temple. "I just want to soak in the hot tub," she groaned.

Amber almost laughed out loud at Clarissa's pathetic acting and even more so at the look Seth exchanged with Matt.

Matt appealed to Shane and Tawnya. "Come on, you guys want to go, don't you?"

"Not really," Shane said. "I think dessert is a good choice."

They only had the limo until midnight, so they went to Matt's house where Shane had left his car, and Amber and Seth rode with Matt and Clarissa to the place they had decided on. Shane and Tawnya followed them. Matt gave Seth the silent treatment on the way there, but after they ordered their dessert and Seth and Shane started talking, Matt rejoined the conversation, and they had a great time— everyone except Clarissa who sat there looking bored and kept complaining about her headache.

Shortly before one o'clock, Shane and Tawnya decided they'd better go. They all left the table together and said good-bye to Shane and Tawnya in the parking lot. Seth and Amber got into Matt's car, and Matt headed for Seth's house, but Seth stopped him when he went to turn onto the street heading up the hill.

"Isn't Clarissa's house that way?" he asked, pointing straight ahead.

"Yes, but I'm taking you two home first."

"No, you're not," Seth said.

Amber expected Matt to argue, but he didn't. When the signal light turned green, Matt went straight instead of turning.

Clarissa stared at him, but Matt didn't look at her. Her house wasn't that far. Matt pulled alongside the curb, didn't say anything, got out of the car, and went around to open Clarissa's door.

Clarissa let out a huff and got out. After Matt closed the door, Seth sighed and leaned his head back. "Thank you, Jesus," he whispered.

Chapter Three

When Matt turned into Seth's driveway, Seth got out of the car and helped her out before closing the door and giving her a light kiss. "I'll just be a few minutes," he said.

Amber squeezed his hand and stepped away, heading for the front door. While they had been waiting for Matt to say good-night to Clarissa, Seth had told her he wanted to talk to Matt when they got here, and she knew that was a good idea, especially since Matt didn't speak a word after returning to the car.

She stepped inside and went into the formal living room to wait for Seth. Kerri appeared a minute later. She was in her pajamas but didn't look like she had been sleeping.

"I thought I heard the front door," she said, coming to sit beside her. "Where's Seth?"

"Out talking to Matt."

"Did anything else happen?"

"Not really," she said, explaining about talking everyone into going out for dessert and then Matt taking Clarissa home first.

"When I heard you might be going to Jake's party, I really started praying," Kerri said. Seth had been keeping in touch with his parents off and on throughout the night and letting them know why they might be later than they had originally planned.

"How did things go with Erin?"

"Great!" Kerri said. "I'm really glad you thought to call me. After we were on our way to her house, she told me she was worried about her mom being mad at her, so we came here for an hour instead, and she opened up to me a lot."

"What did she say?"

"A bunch of different stuff. Her parents are divorced, and that's been hard on her. She moved here with her mom this summer, and she hasn't made many friends yet. And what happened with Pete tonight was definitely not what she was expecting. Pete comes across as being a sweet guy, but he's not. Several of my friends have found that out."

"I could tell she wasn't having a good time from the moment we got into the limo, and it only got worse. That's why I decided to talk to her."

"What made you think to call me?"

"Jesus, I guess."

Kerri smiled. "I believe that! On the way over to her house I told her about our mentoring program, and she said she's heard about it but hadn't signed up, so I offered to be her mentor and she agreed."

"That's great," Amber said, giving Kerri a hug.

"How did Pete take it?"

"Not so good," Amber laughed. "I seriously thought he was going to punch Seth, but he just left. And then when I heard he had gone to the party, I really started praying we wouldn't end up there."

"Poor Seth," Kerri laughed. "He's got the heart of a warrior and the body of—well, Seth."

Amber laughed. "Fortunately, with Jesus on his side, that's all he needs."

They heard Seth come in, and they both tried to hide their laughter. Kerri got up to give him a hug when he stepped into the room, and she told him how proud she was of him.

"Thanks," he said.

Kerri said she was going to bed, and Seth told her 'good night'. Amber said she would be up in a few minutes and waited for Seth to come sit beside her.

"How did things go with Matt?"

"Okay," he said. "I talked to him about Clarissa, and he admitted he's not really dating her because he enjoys it. It's more about being with a girl like her—pretty and popular."

"Is he going to break up with her?"

"Probably. I told him there are more girls like you out there than he thinks, and that any of them would be very fortunate to have him—If he acts like himself instead of what you saw tonight, and you know what he told me?"

"What?"

Seth smiled. "He said, 'I kept wishing Amber was my date instead of Clarissa.'"

"He did not."

"Yes, Amber. He did. He thought you looked really beautiful, not to mention the fact you're a million times more fun to be around than girls like Clarissa." Seth leaned over and kissed her. "Thanks for being my girl."

She smiled and enjoyed one more kiss before Seth said he needed to go talk to his dad.

"Do you think he's still up?"

"I'm sure he is."

"Is he going to be mad we were out so late?"

"No, but he'll want to know more details than I was able to give him over the phone."

Seth helped her up. "Feel free to sleep in tomorrow," he said. "I'm sure I will."

She kissed him at the base of the stairs before she went up to Kerri's room to get out of her dress and then went to the bathroom to wash her face and brush her teeth. By the time she returned, Kerri was asleep, and she got into the large bed quietly and thought about the evening. It hadn't turned out exactly the way she'd imagined but had definitely been memorable.

She and Seth did have nice moments in the midst of it all. She felt more in love with him after seeing him stand up to his friends. She knew how difficult that could be, and she also knew it wasn't the first time he had done so.

In the morning they did sleep in, but they were up and ready in time to go to the eleven o'clock church service. She enjoyed the modern worship songs they sang in the large auditorium, and she also enjoyed the pastor's message. With Christmas coming up in another three weeks, he talked about what an amazing thing God had done by coming to earth to become one of us.

"How can anyone say, 'God doesn't care'? He came, He died, He paid the ultimate price to rescue us!

"How can anyone say, 'Well, maybe God exists, but I don't need Him'? Without Him we are nothing. We're lost. We don't even know where we're supposed to be going, let alone how to get there.

"How can anyone say, 'What does it matter how I live as long as I end up in Heaven in the end anyway?'

"Oh, people, hear me when I say this: God has so much in store for us right here on Planet Earth. In the wonderful fabric of our lives that He can weave together so perfectly when we let Him. Don't let Jesus' sacrifice be in vain. He came for you. He came to restore you. To restore your heart, your family, your past hurts; He came to restore us to wholeness and to live—not just after this life is over, but right here, right now. To live in freedom and abundance and the reality of His all-consuming love.

"Live with the knowledge that you are loved. That you matter to God. That you matter to those around you. With Jesus your life can be radically different. It can be good. It can be free of guilt and shame and regret. It can be filled with beauty. It can be worth living."

Seth had made a point to find Matt this morning and sit beside him. Clarissa wasn't there, at least not that Amber saw. During the final song, Amber had her eyes closed and was singing from her heart when she felt Seth step away from her. Opening her eyes, she saw Seth sitting down beside Matt who had his face in his hands and appeared to be crying.

Amber kept singing and let Seth handle it. By the time they were dismissed, Seth was praying with Matt, and she and Kerri remained in their chairs talking with each other until Seth and Matt were finished. Amber couldn't hear what they were saying, just the soft murmur of their voices, but when they finished, they both stood up and Matt hugged Seth.

"You never give up on me, do you?" Matt said.

"The day I give up on my friends is the day God gives up on me."

In that moment Amber realized something. During the week she had been at camp and first met Seth, he had sat behind her during one of the Fireside meetings, and after Scooby had shared his testimony, she had seen Seth being supportive of the friend sitting beside him. She just now made the connection it had been Matt.

He looked different now. Taller, broader, and very good-looking. She had always thought so since officially meeting him sometime last year. She thought of girls like Kerri and Erin and those in her own youth group who were looking for guys like Seth, and she knew Matt was one of them. He just needed the right girl to bring all of his good qualities to the surface instead of dragging him down like Clarissa.

They went out to lunch with Matt and then returned to Seth's house briefly to get her things before Seth drove her home. He needed to be back for youth group tonight, and she had homework to do, so he didn't stay too long. When he kissed her good-bye outside the front door, he apologized once more for how last night had turned out.

"I'd say everything turned out rather well," she said. "And you can tell Matt I'm going to be praying for a good girl for him."

Seth smiled. "I'll tell him he'd better watch out. My God listens to my girl."

Chapter Four

After watching Seth drive away and stepping into the house, Amber went to the living room where her parents were relaxing and told them the complete story of what had happened last night. They had known about the change in plans with the limo and everything, and she and Seth had briefly shared the evening involved a few interesting twists but everything had turned out all right in the end.

But Amber wanted to brag on Seth more than he would ever brag on himself, and she told them everything he had said and done, and also about Matt this morning. Her mother, in turn, couldn't resist sharing about a time when they'd been in college and her dad had gone to a party to keep his roommate from doing something stupid and dragged him out of there half-drunk after his friend hit him in the face.

When Amber saw that look in her mother's eyes she knew well, she excused herself from the room and went upstairs to do her homework. But she had to smile. She loved seeing her parents still in love with each other. It made her believe she and Seth could spend the rest of their lives together and still be happy twenty years from now, as long as they kept following God's ways and the plans He had for them like she knew her parents had.

She told the whole story once again to Stacey and Nicole after Bible study that night. "I can't believe your parents actually let you go," Nicole said.

"What makes you say that?"

"I don't know, they seem so strict sometimes. I can't believe they let you be out past midnight."

"I don't think of them as being strict. I think of them as being protective and trusting me to make good choices but providing boundaries at the same time."

"So why the sudden change where they're fine with letting you ride in a limo with people you don't know and stay out however long it would have been necessary for the sake of Seth's friends?"

"Because they trust Seth to take care of me, I guess," she said, realizing how true that must be. She hadn't thought about it before, but when she told her parents about the limo and going with Seth's friends, they didn't tell her she needed to be back at Seth's by any certain time. They had left that completely up to Seth and whatever his parents decided would be appropriate.

When she got home, she decided to call him, and they talked for an hour. Some about the weekend but mostly about the things they normally talked about: what they had done since seeing each other this afternoon, what their coming week looked like and their plans for next weekend, what they'd been learning in their individual quiet times, and they both commented on the pastor's message from this morning.

"I think we're living like that, don't you?" she asked him.

"Yes."

They were both quiet for a moment and then Seth asked if Ben was coming home this week. "Yes, on Thursday," she replied.

"I definitely want to spend some time with Ben and Hope while they're here," he said. "Of all the things I enjoyed about this summer, spending time with them was just about the best thing."

She had enjoyed that too. "And what was the absolute best thing?" she asked him.

"Seeing you every day."

"Yeah?"

"No contest, sweetheart."

"Are you still planning on going back next summer?"

"At this point, yes."

"Me too," she said. "And I'm definitely thinking of applying to be a counselor. Is that all right with you?"

"I think that's where you belong."

"It will mean less time together."

"Yes, but I think it's worth it."

"Are you thinking of counseling too?"

"Yes."

"You will be an awesome counselor," she said. "And you're right, it will be worth it. I still think about those girls a lot."

"And I'm sure they still think of you. You're a natural. You fit perfectly into that role."

Seth's words warmed her heart, and she liked him seeing her that way. "Thanks," she said. "It's good to know I'm good at something besides sports."

"You're good at a lot of things besides sports, Amber. Not the least of which the way you love people, including me."

"Now you're going to make me cry," she said, seriously feeling tears welling up in her eyes.

"And you could cry a river, because it's the truth."

"Thank you, Seth. That means a lot coming from you."

"I've gotten so used to thinking of you that way, I'd almost forgotten how different you are from a lot of girls. Last night was a good reality-check for me. I've gotten used to seeing girls at school who dress or act a certain way, and I've learned to mostly ignore it and not let it affect me, but seeing

Clarissa hanging all over one of my best friends and dragging him down was different. I can't even imagine being with someone like that. Thank you, Amber, for being exactly who you are."

"And seeing Erin with Pete was a good reality-check for me, Seth. When we first met, I was very naive about the way guys could be, and I'm so thankful you're not that way."

She also told him about what Nicole had said earlier and that it made her realize how much her parents had come to trust him. "And I trust you too, Seth. I didn't have any reason to believe I had anything to worry about, even if we would have gone to that party. You always take care of me no matter where we are or who we're with."

"I can't imagine doing anything else. I had a dream a few weeks ago where we had broken up and you were with this other guy who didn't treat you well, and I kept following you and pleading with you to get away from him. When I woke up, my heart was pounding, and I knew what it would feel like to see anyone hurting you in any way. I was furious, Amber. I mean it. I've never had such angry feelings as I had for this imaginary guy."

"I guess Jesus rescued us both, huh? Even before we knew we needed to be rescued."

"Yes, He did," he said softly.

She hated to say it, but glancing at the time, she knew she should. "I think I'm going to say good-night now."

"That's a good note to end on," he said. "I'll be thinking about that for days."

"Me too. I love you."

"I love you too, sweetheart. Good night."

Amber thought about that for the next couple of days. It seemed like whenever she began to wonder if she was on the right path and if her life was really any different because of the way she was choosing to live it, God brought significant moments and the words of others that confirmed what she knew to be true:

The way God said to live was right. It made her different. It made her happy. It gave her peace. And it also made a difference for those around her. She wasn't lost; she was living life the way it was meant to be lived. And that was a great feeling. And it also confirmed the profound reality that she was loved by God. He valued her. She wasn't a cosmic accident or one of the masses. He knew her. He called her by name. He had a plan specifically designed just for her. She had no reason to fear. She could trust Him to take care of her—always.

On Tuesday night they had a home basketball game, and she actually got to play quite a bit. Her coach needed her in there on defense, she told her, and Amber played her heart out—stealing balls and knocking them away right and left, leaping for rebounds and getting fouled several times in the process, giving her the chance to shoot free-throws and score key points for their team.

Even though she had told her parents they didn't need to come to her games, she was glad to see her dad arrive just after half-time. Coach Hathaway had put her in halfway through the second quarter when they were getting creamed, and her coach had her start the second half and kept her in for the majority of the rest of the game as they managed to catch up and win by three points.

"Great game, sweetheart," her dad said, giving her a hug. "You haven't been playing that much and we've been missing it, have you?"

"No," she laughed. "It was all working tonight, and I guess the coach thought so too."

"Great game, Ambs," she heard Stacey say.

She turned to compliment Stacey on her good play as well and then told her good-night, saying she wouldn't need a ride home.

"Okay, see you tomorrow."

Turning back to her dad, Amber took the warm-up jacket she had handed him and put it on over her uniform and then walked out of the gymnasium beside him, saying good-night to other teammates along the way.

When they reached the van, they got inside and Amber put on her seat-belt, but her dad didn't start the motor. He put the keys into the ignition and turned to face her.

"I have some bad news, Jewel."

She looked at him and froze. She knew he was serious, and his somewhat subdued mood suddenly seemed so obvious. He hadn't been himself even while he'd been sitting in the stands, she realized.

"What?" she asked in a soft voice.

"Your grandpa had a heart attack this afternoon."

"Grandpa Smith?" she asked, referring to her grandparents who lived here in Sandy.

"Yes," he confirmed.

"Is he okay?"

"No," he said, swallowing hard but not looking away from her. "He died. When Grandma went to wake him up from his afternoon nap, he was already gone."

Amber felt like a piece of her heart had been cut out. She felt too numb to cry. Her dad leaned over and took her into his arms. *Grandpa gone?* She couldn't fathom it. Her grandparents had always been here, living close by. She had afternoon lunch with them almost every Sunday. Her grandfather wasn't a big talker, but he was sweet and loving and always there. How could he be gone?

"Where's Mom?"

"With Grandma. We're going to be taking her home with us tonight, and she'll probably stay with us for a few days."

Amber's heart broke for her grandmother. She and Grandpa had been married for more than fifty years. They had started dating when they were teenagers. They had gotten married when they were twenty. He was her first and only love. Her soul-mate. The first and only boy she had ever kissed. She started crying at the thought.

Her dad held her until she quieted down. The tears were still flowing as they drove the short distance to her grandparents' home. She could barely get out of the van and walk up the front steps of the house, knowing her grandfather would not be there.

He'd had a minor heart attack last Christmas, nearly a year ago, but he'd had surgery and the doctors had said he would be all right. At the time she remembered wondering how she would feel if he hadn't made it, but she had never imagined this. She felt absolutely empty and sadder than she had ever felt in her life.

Stepping inside the house ahead of her dad, she walked into the kitchen where she could hear voices, and she saw her mother, Aunt Dawn, and her grandmother sitting at the kitchen table. Her mom appeared to have been crying recently, but Grandma looked up and smiled.

Amber walked over, and her grandmother rose to meet her. She hugged her warmly and fresh tears began to flow. "I'm sorry, Grandma."

Her grandmother held her tight for several moments and then released her. Amber felt perplexed by the peaceful expression on her face. She appeared sad but not mournful. Maybe she was still in shock and the reality hadn't sunk in yet. But her words told her otherwise.

"He's where he has always longed to be, princess," she said with calmness and certainty. "He's with Jesus now."

Chapter Five

Amber didn't go to school in the morning, and she continued to feel numb and hollow for most of the day, but she also learned more reasons why her grandmother had such peace. While her parents went to make funeral arrangements, she remained at the house with Grandma and had a chance to talk with her at length. Her grandmother wanted to hear all about her time at the dance, and then Amber continued telling her other things about herself and Seth, their relationship and plans, and how fortunate she felt to have him in her life.

Her grandmother told her more stories about when she and Grandpa had been young, and even though she had tears in her eyes several times, she also had that look of peace and a smile on her face too.

"He's been in a lot of pain the last few months, sweetie," her grandmother informed her. "I know he never complained about it, but his arthritis had been bothering him something terrible. His medicine stopped working, and he couldn't keep up with the vegetable garden this summer. And then he had to stop delivering meals once the cold weather came because he couldn't get in and out of the van that much. I'll miss him terribly, but knowing he's not in that pain anymore will get me through this."

Amber hugged her once again, more for herself than for her grandmother. Her grandmother may have been expecting this to some extent, but she hadn't. Grandpa wasn't a complainer. He had seemed perfectly healthy a week ago when she had been there listening to her grandmother tell her story. He'd been outside part of the time, fixing the latch on the front gate, and then had come inside and sat and listened to his beloved wife share about that special time all those years ago.

"Are you going to stay here and live with us?" she asked.

"I don't know about that yet," her grandmother replied. "I have good neighbors I know will watch out for me, and I have a lot of things to do at the church—I'm there just about every day, it seems. That would be a lot of driving back and forth from here."

Amber knew her grandmother could take care of herself, and she was very healthy and active, but Amber had a difficult time imagining her living all alone in that house without Grandpa.

"I'll come stay with you sometimes," she said. "I could sleep-in another twenty minutes before I'd have to get up and go to school."

Her grandmother laughed. "You do that, princess. I'd love it."

Amber didn't try to call Seth that evening. She would have liked to talk to him, but he had swim practice after school and then had Bible study with the leadership team on Wednesday nights and usually didn't get home until after nine.

On Thursday he had a swim meet, so she didn't try calling until after she knew he would be home from that. She managed to tell him the news without crying. Some of the shock had worn off, and Grandma's good spirits had rubbed off on her after spending the past two days with her. Ben had come home that evening also, and having everyone together, reminding her of what a close-knit family she had, had helped her to feel more settled.

Seth expressed his sympathy for her loss. One of his grandfathers had died when he was thirteen, so he understood the feelings she was having. He offered to come out for the memorial service scheduled for Saturday morning.

"Don't you have to work?" she asked. During swim season he wasn't able to work after school, so he often worked on Saturday mornings, but he hadn't last Saturday because of the dance, and the weekend before he'd been here also.

"I'm scheduled to, but I can call Mr. Davidson. He'll understand. If you want me there, that's where I want to be, Amber."

"I want you here," she whispered, feeling the tears returning once again.

"Would you like some happy news?" he asked.

"I'd love some happy news."

"I have two things, actually," he said. "Matt broke up with Clarissa on Monday. And, I talked to him after Bible study last night about the possibility of going to Lifegate with us next year and being my roommate, and he said he'd think about it."

"That's great," she said.

"I thought you'd like that."

"You and my grandpa are a lot alike," she said.

"Oh yeah?"

"Yes. I've been thinking that since I heard the story about their first dance together, and hearing Grandma talk about him so much these past couple of days has made me think so even more."

"I want to read that story you wrote," he said.

"I'll print another copy, and you can read it on Saturday."

"Have you shared it with your family?"

"Not yet. I barely got it done on time and then with the dance and everything last weekend, I forgot about it."

"You should read it to everyone. Your grandmother would love it, I'm sure. Especially now."

She knew he was probably right. "Okay, I'll do that." She was about to let him go, knowing he had homework to get done, but then she thought to ask how his swim meet had gone.

For as interested and supportive as he always was about her games and matches, she knew her efforts paled in comparison. He had told her she didn't need to be there because he only swam in three events: the 50 freestyle, the 100 freestyle, and the freestyle relay, which all were fast races. The rest of the time she had to just sit there and watch a bunch of people swim she didn't know. But she did always try to ask him about it, and that answer was usually the same. He almost always took first or second place, and his relay team always won.

Tonight his answer was slightly different, and she was glad she'd thought to ask because Seth would never have told her otherwise. "I took first place in both of my individual races, our relay team won, and I set a new school record in the 100."

"You did!" She felt excited for him. He'd been chasing that goal for a long time. "That's great. I'm happy for you."

"It was a pretty great feeling," he said. "But you know what?"

"What?"

"It doesn't compare to how I feel every time you smile at me."

She smiled.

"I wish I could see that one on your face right now."

"You can see it on Saturday."

"Promise? It can't be just a sad day. Your grandpa is with Jesus, after all."

"I promise," she said. "Just a few tears."

"I love you, Amber. I love you. I love you. I love you."

"I love you too, Seth. Thanks for talking. I'll see you on Saturday."

Amber was amazed by how much lighter her heart felt after talking with Seth. She finished up her homework and got into bed, reading the letter she had gotten from him today but saved until now.

When she had called him earlier, he had asked if she'd gotten one today, and she told him she had but hadn't read it yet. He said he thought maybe that's why she was calling, so she wondered if there might be something particularly special he had said.

She was right. He had written her a brief note about what a great time he'd had at the dance, and the second page had a poem he had written for her. Of all days, she knew she could use one of his sweet poems right now, and she cherished every word as if it was the first one he had ever written for her.

The Dance

The dance had music and colorful lights
It was a magical, memorable, somewhat crazy night
But she was simply gorgeous, a beautiful sight
I just wanted to kiss her and hold her tight

All night I kept thinking what had brought us to this place
Whoever thought spilled Pepsi could bring about such grace
She's changed my heart, my life, my view of time and space
And to think I've just started, just had a little taste

Of her sweetness and her light, of her love and of her joy
Of the love that can pass between this girl and this boy
Of the sweetness of her lips, of the way she makes me feel
Of the life we'll live together, so right and so real

It was only a dance, just a small point in time
And yet I know I won't forget, sweet Amber of mine
The memories will follow me my whole life through
And I hope with all my heart you'll remember it too

Remember it with joy, remember it with peace
Remember with a smile upon your pretty face
Remember who held you close and hopes you remember
That he loves you very much, always and forever

She had a special place she kept the poems Seth had written her, and she got out of bed to get them out of her desk. Looking at each one, she read her favorite last. *Two Seeking Hearts* had not only been a great poem but had also become something she defined their relationship by.

Two seeking hearts are stronger than one
And it's hard to believe that He's only begun
To weave our hearts together into one, don't you see?
I believe that's what He's doing between you and me

I never imagined it would be like this
So pure and right, nothing but bliss
You're invading my heart so easy and fast
And I hope and pray the blue skies will last

We'll seek Him together, not just apart
We'll share our thoughts, we'll share our hearts
We'll learn His truth and live it out
I want us to shine and maybe even shout

That His love is real and it is here
Within our hearts it becomes clear
This isn't a mistake or just random chance
He wants us to live, He wants us to dance

And so we will dance, my jewel, my treasure
Not with meaningless talk and mere fleeting pleasure
But by seeking things above: His love and His heart
Yes, Amber, I believe this is only the start

And Seth had been exactly right. They'd known each other only a few weeks when he'd written that, and yet more than a year later they were still living the same way. They had both grown tremendously in their relationship with God and with each other, and yet the principles behind what made both work didn't change. Seeking God. Seeking truth. Seeking whatever God had for them in this dance called life.

Before going to sleep, she wrote a letter to Seth, thanking him for his most recent poem, reminding him of the other one, and expressing her thoughts on that. She ended the letter by saying:

If I had to live the last year over again, I wouldn't change a thing. I am very happy with the way we are choosing to live, and I'm so thankful you are willing to walk this path with me. Side by side. Hand in hand. Laughing, loving, praying, learning, and dancing together. Let's not stop now, sweet thing. I love you. I love you. I love you.

Always,
Amber

Chapter Six

Amber returned to school on Friday so she wouldn't get too far behind, and for the most part she had a good day. Her friends had heard about her grandfather, and they were all sympathetic and supportive. She clung to their strength and felt amazed by how much they were there for her and genuinely concerned. On the way home after basketball practice, she thanked Stacey for her support throughout the day and for being the one to spread the word so all of her friends already knew and she didn't have to keep telling everyone all day that her grandpa had died.

"Like you haven't been there for me a million times," Stacey said. "It's nice to be there for you for once."

"You've been there for me plenty, Stace. I've been meaning to thank you for talking me into playing basketball this year. I've been having so much fun. Even having practice today helped with what's going on right now."

"It's good to have you back. That new girl who played your position in volleyball this year was good, but it wasn't like having you there. You're not just a good player, you're fun to play with."

She knew Stacey had no idea how much she needed to hear that, and she didn't say anything, but she took the reality of their friendship deeper into her heart.

"Is Kenny back?" she asked, suddenly remembering he could be.

Stacey smiled. "He came home last night, and he was waiting for me at the school when we got back from the game. We didn't have much time together, but he drove me home, and it was really good to see him."

"Are you going out tonight?"

"Yes. He might be at my house by the time I get there."

"Are you planning to do anything special while he's home?"

"We haven't talked about it, but I'm sure he would like to get together with you and Seth sometime."

"We'll be sure and plan something. This weekend isn't too great, obviously, and next weekend I'm going to that wedding, but maybe during break we can find time."

"How about you and Seth? Any special plans for Christmas and everything?"

"Seth's family is going to California over Christmas, which I was sort of bummed about before, but now that my grandpa is gone I think it will be good to have that time with my family."

"When are your mom and dad going to be officially taking over the youth group?"

"They're planning a Christmas party at our house next Sunday, and then we're going Christmas caroling the following week. And they'll be taking over teaching and everything else after the first of the year."

They had reached her house, and Stacey gave her another hug and told her she would be praying for her.

"Thanks, Stace. See you Sunday."

She got out of the car and went inside, finding everyone there, including Hope, whom she hadn't seen since Thanksgiving. They exchanged a warm hug, and Hope's love and concern was evident. Almost every time someone had hugged her today, she had been reminded of her grandpa. He gave the best hugs. She hadn't thought about it much before, but she remembered that about him now—one more thing that made her realize how much he and Seth were alike.

After hugging her grandmother and her mom and asking how they were doing, she invited Hope to come up to her room while she changed and took a breather from the busy day. As sympathetic as her friends were over her loss, her teachers hadn't relieved her of any of the extra work she had to make up, and she wasn't sure she would have time to do it all this weekend. School felt like an inconvenient burden right now.

Hope wanted to know how the dance had gone, and Amber told her all about it, including what she had told Erin and encouraging her to leave early with Kerri. Hope thought that was very cool and was glad to hear someone else could learn from her mistakes instead of having to make them too.

Hope was supposed to tell her hello from a bunch of people at Western: Lora, Julia, Kyle, Tamara, Lexi, and Josh. She missed them all and hoped they would be at Kyle and Julia's wedding next Saturday along with others from camp.

"How's Lora doing? Do you know?"

"Okay, I think," Hope said. "I actually haven't seen her too much with her and Julia living off campus this year, but whenever I've seen her and Eric at church they've seemed fine. Not quite like they were before, but I overheard her and Tamara talking this last Sunday and Lora said she feels like Winter Break will be a good chance for them to talk and work some things out. I think they've both been really busy this term."

"Yeah, that's what Lora said in one of her letters."

She hadn't been thinking about her the last few days, but ever since she had received her previous letter two weeks ago Lora had been heavy on her heart. Hope's words confirmed that not all was well.

"Could we pray for her and Eric? I don't know if they're meant to be together or not, but if they are and things still aren't right between them, I think only God can make it work."

Hope agreed and they spent a few minutes praying together. After they finished, she asked Hope how things were going for her and Ben, and Hope responded with a smile and simple words. "I'm in love with him, Amber, and I don't see that changing anytime soon."

Amber heard footsteps on the stairs, followed by Ben's familiar knock on her door. She invited him inside, and he came in to tell them they were all getting ready to go to a nearby restaurant for dinner.

"Did you tell her?" Ben said before they left the room.

"Tell her what?" Hope asked.

"About your decision."

"Oh, no. I didn't."

"What decision?" Amber asked.

"You know how I haven't been sure about what I want to major in?"

"Yes."

"After rooming with Lexi and hearing about all the special help she received in school, I had been thinking about going into special education, and then last week I went to one of Lexi's classes with her because they were going to be talking about all the different fields within special education you can specialize in. One of the areas there is a high demand for is sign-language teachers and interpreters for deaf children who are mainstreamed in school, and something about that really appealed to me, so I'm going to start heading that direction and see if it might be for me."

"That sounds cool. I can see you doing that."

Amber thought it was great Hope may have found her career path, but the way Ben seemed so excited for her made her smile even more. *And he's in love with you, Hope, and I don't see that changing anytime soon either.*

Amber enjoyed having dinner with everyone and sat next to her grandmother during the meal. Grandma seemed a little sadder tonight than she had thus far, and Amber could imagine she must be missing Grandpa very much by now. Several times today Amber had almost forgotten her grandfather was gone, and then when it hit she would never see him again this side of heaven, it was like hearing the news for the first time all over again. She supposed her grandmother had experienced that a few times herself.

By the time they returned to the house, Amber felt ready to go upstairs and have a good cry over it. She hadn't wanted to cry at the restaurant, although a few times she had let tears fall. If her grandmother or her mom even had a hint of tears in their eyes—that was too much for her to bear. Riding in the van beside her mom so Grandma could sit up front, Amber didn't see Seth's car until her dad said something and drew her attention to it.

"Did he say he was coming tonight?" her mom asked.

"No," she said, feeling the tears about to spill over any second.

Her grandmother turned around with a sweet smile on her face and patted her knee. "Your grandpa always loved a good surprise too, princess."

At that point she lost it. Her family got out of the van, and Seth stepped over to say hello, hugging her mom and her grandmother warmly and then getting inside the van to sit beside her as the others stepped away toward the house.

He pulled her into his arms, and she laid her head on his shoulder, crying her eyes out. She wasn't sure why. He didn't tell her not to, or say anything at all, but he held her for several minutes, stroking her hair and rubbing her back.

She finally stopped enough to ask him what he was doing here. And he said he felt like he needed to come.

"How long have you been waiting?"

"Twenty minutes," he said. "I would have waited a lot longer. When my Jesus says, 'She needs you, Seth', I'm there."

He kissed her tenderly several times, each one comforting her in a way she felt certain no one else could and also reminding her of the sweet love her grandparents had shared for many years. She hadn't thought of it before, but ever since hearing her grandmother's story, and after hearing her share many fun and special memories the past few days, there was no doubt in her mind that her grandparents had fallen in love all those years ago like she and Seth were doing now.

Oh, God. If I could have this incredibly special person for the rest of my life, I would be so blessed. Please don't take him away. I love him. I need him. I know that together we can shine brightly for you, and that's what I want.

"It's going to be okay, Amber," he spoke softly. "Your grandma will be all right. God knows what He's doing."

His truthful and soothing words calmed her, and she enjoyed his presence, allowing his love to fill up the empty space her grandpa's absence had left.

"Thanks for being here," she said. "I've been doing all right, but my grandma was sad tonight, and that's hard for me to see."

"I'm sure it is," he said. "How long were they married?"

She told him that and a bunch of little things her grandmother had shared the past few days. She told him what her grandma said when they'd driven up and seen him waiting, and they both laughed. It felt good to laugh. Her grandpa had always enjoyed a good joke or funny story, and she had vivid memories of him smiling and laughing, and often it was her grandmother who had made him do so.

"I told Grandma I'd read the story tonight," she said. "I should probably go inside and do that."

"Yes, you should," Seth said, giving her one more kiss and then getting out of the van and waiting for her to follow.

They walked to his car, and Seth got his bag and backpack out before they went into the house. On their way inside, Seth asked if he would have a place to sleep tonight, and she told him her grandmother had been sleeping in Ben's room, so Ben had slept in the living room last night, and he could sleep there too, like he usually did.

"Sweet. We can play video games until Ben begs for mercy."

She laughed. "I'm telling him you said that."

Seth set his bags by the door once they were inside and retracted his optimism. "No, don't tell him," he laughed, pulling her back toward him.

"What will you give to keep me quiet?"

"A thousand kisses," he whispered, giving her one right there.

"A thousand? That may take you awhile to pay off."

He smiled and kissed her again. "I've got time."

He gave her a few more and then Amber felt her dad's presence sneaking up on them. Turning her face away from Seth, she smiled.

"Hi, Daddy." She giggled and defended her boyfriend. "He owes me a thousand kisses."

"Oh yeah? A thousand, huh?"

Seth cleared his throat and spoke most respectfully. "Yes, Sir. I wouldn't want to be slow about repaying my debt, Mr. Wilson—Sir."

Her dad smiled. "You know, I owed Mrs. Wilson a million kisses once. I'm still working to pay that one off." He turned away and spoke over his shoulder. "As you were, Seth. Sorry to interrupt."

Amber looked back to Seth and laughed. He smiled and then spoke seriously. "It's okay for you to be sad, sweetheart. Whenever you need to cry, go right ahead. But if I'm going to live up to being anything like your grandpa, I'm going to have to make you smile, because that's what I remember about him. He always made you smile."

Chapter Seven

Everyone gathered in the living room to listen to Amber share her story, and she felt nervous at first, but once she started speaking and heard the words flowing easily from her lips, she relaxed and hoped her grandmother enjoyed it. She also hoped she could get through it without crying. There were parts that brought tears to her eyes now that Grandpa was gone.

"Are you going to the dance, Dottie?"

I replied without looking up from my book. "No, Shirley. I told you that already."

"Why not? Come on. It will be fun."

"I'm not going without a date!"

Shirley came to sit beside me on the porch swing. I reluctantly moved over to give her more space. "Lots of girls will be there who don't have a date. That's part of why we have dances—to meet boys, not just dance with someone you already know."

I finally looked up from my book. "But you're going with Marvin, Peggy is going with Jim, and Fern is going with Max. I would be the only one there by myself, and I don't want any charity dances with Marvin and all my girlfriends' beaus. I'm not going!"

"Okay, okay. Sorry I brought it up."

I went back to my reading, feeling quite proud of myself for not letting Shirley have her way. I had lived in my older sister's shadow long enough—doing whatever she wanted, whatever she talked me into. Well, not anymore. I was sixteen now, almost seventeen. And I didn't need a beau to take me to some silly dance. I wanted to go to college after all. Shirley and Marvin were getting married this summer, and I thought it was ridiculous. I wasn't going to be falling for some boy who would put an end to my dreams and plans. No way.

"You could always ask someone," Shirley piped in once again. "Lots of girls are doing that now. It's perfectly acceptable. Some boys are shy and need a little persuasion."

"I'm not interested in anyone. And even if I was, I don't think it's right to be the one asking. If a boy is too shy to ask, he needs to grow up a little."

"Oh, Dot. Don't be so melodramatic," Shirley said, rising from the swing with a swish of her pink skirt. "Fine, go ahead and read your books and go to college and die an old-maid. What do I care?"

"Just because I don't go to the spring dance doesn't mean I'll die an old maid. I'm waiting for a mature, smart, rich, college graduate. Someone just like me when I'm twenty-five. I don't think any girl should get married until at least then."

"Whatever you say, bookworm. But the day a girl from this Podunk town graduates from college will be the day a girl gets married who refused to snatch up a boy before they're all taken. That's not the way it works"

"It will work for me."

From that day on I vowed to make Shirley eat her words. I would go to college. I would get a degree in something very prestigious. And I would marry a handsome man. A doctor or a lawyer or a successful businessman. That's what I was waiting for, not just some boy from my hometown who worked at the garage or the diner or would take over his daddy's farm. Un-huh. This girl was going places.

Everyone laughed as Amber paused. She looked at her grandmother and could see tears glistening in her eyes. But not sad tears like earlier. Joyful ones from the memory of this special time in her life that hadn't turned out the way she had planned it, but exactly the way she would choose to do it all over again.

Amber also glanced at Seth, and his loving gaze encouraged her to keep reading. She couldn't believe she had the ability to write like this. She didn't plan anything in advance, and the words seemed to come out of nowhere once she got started. She had written this story in one afternoon and thought she would have to make a bunch of revisions to have it ready to turn in the following day, but other than a few minor changes, this is the way it had come out originally.

Two weeks went by and no invitation to the dance came. Secretly I did think it would be nice to go and show Shirley I could attract a boy's eye the same as she could, but if it didn't happen I wasn't going to get all bent out of shape. It would probably turn out to be boring anyway. How much fun could it be to dance for two hours and drink watered-down punch? Especially if my toes kept getting stepped on like with that boy at my cousin's wedding last summer. I only danced with him once, and my feet hurt for two days.

But still, I found myself keeping an ear out, wondering if Robert or Winston had asked anyone yet. They were two boys I knew from church, whom I had always been a little sweet on, but on the Sunday before the dance neither of them even looked my way during the service. It was just as well. Winston's father owned the Five and Dime store and Robert's daddy was a pig farmer. I'd never get out of town with either of them taking my hand.

I knew the possibility that I would be going to the dance with my sister and friends ended at that point. Robert and Winston were the only boys from our small church who didn't already have dates, and I knew Mama and Papa wouldn't let me go with any boy who didn't attend church. I faced the week feeling determined to go about my normal business, casually telling others I wasn't planning to go to the dance when they asked, and doing my best to ignore all the colorful posters in the hallways and the ticket-sale booth set up outside the cafeteria.

The worst was over by Wednesday. Shirley finally stopped pestering me about asking Robert or Winston myself, and my friends were too focused on their own last-minute preparations to think about my lonely plight. Not that I was lonely, mind you. My books and porch swing kept me company, and my mama needed extra help with cooking and such with Shirley off to this place or that after school every day.

I didn't see Charlie Smith walk up the front path that evening until he was at the base of the steps.

His presence startled me because I wasn't expecting anyone to be standing there when I lifted my eyes from my book at the end of a particularly thrilling chapter.

"Oh, Charlie. You scared me," I laughed. "Don't sneak up on me like that."

"Sorry, Dorothy," he said, walking up the steps and onto the front porch. "I thought you would hear me coming up the walk. That must be a good book."

"Yes," I said, lowering it to my lap and asking Charlie what he was doing here. He often came by to do odd jobs for my papa since his back had been bothering him so. But he had been here yesterday, helping Papa plant the vegetable garden, and he usually only came by on Tuesdays and Thursdays, not Wednesdays.

"May I sit down?" he asked.

"Oh, sure," I said, moving over on the porch swing so he would have plenty of room.

"I probably should have asked you this sooner, Dorothy," he said, giving me a shy smile. "But I didn't think I would be able to go because my grandfather has his bowling league on Friday nights and I've been driving him since his eyesight at night has gotten bad."

I didn't know why Charlie was telling me all this or have any idea what he thought he should have asked me sooner. But I kept silent and waited for him to get around to the reason he had stopped by. Perhaps this had something to do with the church picnic coming up in a few weeks. The youth had been asked to run some games for the children, and Shirley and I had been put in charge of it. As the pastor's daughters we were usually the ones called upon to organize any activities or special events for the young people.

Charlie was one of the youth boys too, but I didn't always think of him as being my age. His parents had died of a bad fever when he was young, and he had been raised by his grandparents. A few years back his grandmother had gone to be with Jesus too, and it was just him and his grandfather now. They were there every Sunday, but Charlie always sat with Grandpa Smith rather than some of the other boys like Robert and Winston. And he seemed much older than me. I wasn't sure why. Maybe because he had been forced to grow up sooner with an ailing grandmother to care for and helping his grandfather run their small farm that my papa said was the worst farming land for miles and miles.

I kept my gaze on Charlie and waited for him to go on. I noticed he still had on his school clothes instead of what I knew he would wear to do his chores after school or to help my papa.

"Haven't you been home yet?" I asked. It was well after supper-time.

"No. I usually go to the library on Wednesdays," he said. "I guess the time got away from me tonight. Grandpa's probably wondering where I am."

"Why do you go to the library?"

"To study."

"Why don't you just study at home?"

"They won't let you check out those big atlases. I can only study them there."

"Oh! You mean the ones with all those pictures and everything?"

"Yes. You've looked at them?"

"I love those. I love seeing all those photographs of cities and rivers and mountains instead of just lines drawn on a map."

"Me too," he said with his brown eyes sparkling. "That's what I want to study when I go to college. Geography is one of the few things that makes sense to me, I think because I can see the maps and the pictures and dream about going to those places someday."

"I didn't know you were planning to go to college. What about your grandfather? Doesn't he need you to stay here?"

"No, he's planning to sell the farm next year and move back to Washington to be near his family. He stayed here for me and will give me the money from the property and everything to go to college. In fact, he's insisting that I go. He wants me to pursue my dreams instead of taking over a farm that isn't much of a farm to begin with. He got suckered into buying that place a long time ago and certainly doesn't want to pass the curse on to me."

"Does he think anyone will want to buy it?"

"Not for farming, but it's got a nice view and lots of trees for someone looking to build a nice home or board horses or some other thing that lots of city-folk are moving out here for. He's already had a couple of good offers, but he wants me to finish high school here. This is where all my friends are—and my memories."

I saw Charlie in a different light that day. He was usually so quiet, but he couldn't seem to stop talking once he got started. I learned his big dreams were to *finish college and become a history or geography teacher and to travel as much as possible over the course of a lifetime. At least to see most of the United States and Canada and then maybe, if he could save enough, to go to Europe someday.*

I had no idea then how much a part of his dreams I would end up being, or what he was about to ask me.

"So anyway," Charlie said, smiling sweetly at me. "When Grandpa heard about the dance from Mrs. Wilkins on Sunday, he asked me if I was going, and when I used his bowling league as my excuse, he insisted on finding a ride some other way, especially when he heard there was a girl I was interested in going with."

I tried to figure out whom Charlie was talking about and why on earth he would be telling me about it, unless he was planning to ask one of my friends and he wanted my opinion on if she would agree to go with him. And other than asking kind of late for a girl to get a new dress and whatever else Shirley and everyone had been doing after school this week, I thought any girl would be very happy to go to a dance with a boy like Charlie. He was very nice and always friendly and pretty swell to look at too, but most of my friends already had been asked, so I felt sort of sorry for him that he might not be able to take whom he would like after all.

When his hand reached across the space between us and he took my fingers into his own, I didn't have a chance to realize what was happening before he spoke. His voice sounded calm but softer than usual, and his words took me by complete surprise.

"I'd like to go with you, Dorothy. Would that be all right?"

I looked into his warm brown eyes and didn't think he could be serious. But if I knew one thing about Charlie Smith, I knew he would never tease a girl about something so serious, let alone do so right there on my daddy's front porch. But how could he want to take me? Because everyone else was already taken? Because Shirley had begged him to ask me?

"I—I don't have anything to wear," I said. "I—I wasn't really—"

"What about that nice dress you were wearing on Easter? You don't need to have a brand new dress, do you?"

"I—I don't know," I said. "I suppose not, but I'm not sure an Easter dress is appropriate—"

"I would be fine with seeing you in it again. Blue is a real nice color on you. Of course, if you'd rather not go with me," he said, taking his hand away, "I can accept that. I didn't mean to assume you—I just thought—I know I haven't really said anything, but I do think you're a real nice girl, Dorothy. But if you don't want to or think you and I—"

His voice trailed off and he seemed embarrassed. He had started to ramble nervously, and I suddenly realized he must have felt this way about me for quite some time. And even though he had never said anything before now, I could see that we had gotten to know each other and become friends over the years. I had been at his grandmother's funeral and felt so bad for him that day. I had made the effort to talk to him more at church and school after that. And since he'd been coming around to help my papa these last few months, he had usually stopped to talk to me on his way out. But this was the first time he had actually sat down next to me either inside or out here on the swing.

"I'd love to go with you, Charlie," I said, realizing how true that was as I spoke the words.

"Really?" he asked, giving me a cautious smile.

"Yes, really." I laughed. "You sort of surprised me or I would have said yes right away. My Easter dress will be fine, and I'm actually glad you waited this long to ask me or I would have fretted about it for weeks."

His expression turned soft, and he took my hand once again, giving my fingers a gentle squeeze and my heart a warm feeling. "No reason to be nervous, Dorothy. I think we'll have a real nice time. I always do when I'm with you."

I'm not sure why, but I believed he was right, and the dance did turn out to be the most special night of my life up to that point. Dancing with him was nice, and we never ran out of things to talk about. When he walked me up the front steps and stood with me on the porch for a few minutes, he was still telling me about faraway places he would like to see, and I was starting to have dreams of being with him when he saw the Grand Canyon and Niagara Falls and The Great Lakes.

I didn't expect him to kiss me good night, but he did. He was the first boy to ever kiss me, and later I learned I was the first girl he ever kissed. We were married three years later, after we had both finished our second year of college. Charlie did become a history and geography teacher at the high school right there in our hometown, but he also took me to see the world.

Chapter Eight

There wasn't a dry eye in the room when Amber finished. Neatly folding the pages, she tucked them into a white envelope and took it to her grandmother, giving her a long hug and handing her the story to keep.

"Thank you, sweetie," her grandmother said. "That was wonderful. Exactly the way I remember it."

"I'm glad," she said. "Thanks for sharing it with me. I thought this would just be an assignment for a class, but I think God had much more in mind."

They all remained in the living room, sharing stories about Grandpa. It was a special time with her family and she was glad Seth was here. She didn't feel embarrassed about leaning into him and letting him hold her as the conversation danced around the room from one story and mood to the next. One minute they were all laughing, and the next they had tears in their eyes.

Once her parents and her grandmother had gone to bed, and Ben had left to take Hope home, she and Seth had a few minutes to themselves at the base of the stairs.

"Your story was really good, Amber," he said. "And this isn't your boyfriend talking; it's someone who knows a lot about writing and weeds through a lot of mediocre articles each week to put in the school paper. I can't believe this is the only writing class you've ever taken. I have classmates who've been in journalism with me since freshman year who don't write that well."

"I think it's a gift, like your acting. I don't work at it, it just happens."

"Then don't stop. After this class is over, you should sit down and write several times a week, just for fun. See what comes out of that pretty head. I could be married to a famous novelist someday."

She appreciated Seth's encouragement and kind words, but she thought he might be dreaming a little big. Changing the subject, she gave him a hug and said, "I'm really glad you drove out tonight. Thank you."

"You're welcome," he said, holding her for a long time.

She enjoyed the extended affection and didn't want to say good-night to him. He only released her enough to exchange his hug for several kisses and told her something that made her laugh.

"I think I just lost count of how many kisses that's been so far. I guess I'll have to start over tomorrow."

He gave her one more before she went up to her room. Getting into bed, she remembered she hadn't done her Bible-reading for today because she had gotten up late this morning. Opening her Bible, she read the verse following the one she had read yesterday and wrote it in her journal at the top of a blank page.

"If the Son sets you free, you will be free indeed."
John 8:36

Amber's thoughts turned to Grandpa. The reality that he was in Heaven with Jesus had changed her perspective of life these last few days. Heaven seemed more real to her than it ever had before. Her grandfather was there instead of here.

Tomorrow, following the memorial service, she would be going to the cemetery to see where his body had been put into the ground, but he wouldn't be there. He was someplace she couldn't see but she knew was real. A place where Grandpa was still very much alive. A place where her grandmother would join him someday and where she herself would also see him again.

I can't imagine not knowing where my grandpa is right now or not knowing where I will go when I die. Thank you, Jesus, for setting us free from the curse of death and for allowing me to know you have done so. I've never really thought about it before, but I have never had a fear of death, and even though Grandpa is gone, I have peace in my heart for him and for Grandma and how she will go on without him. What an incredible thing!

Thank you for also setting me free from the destructive power of sin in my life here and now. The relationship I have with Seth is so valuable and special to me. I can't imagine doing something to spoil it, and by your grace we have managed to remain pure and walk in the path of freedom and joy you have for us. Thank you for also setting me free from fear and worry and the lies of the enemy. I know I don't always live in that freedom. Sometimes I let doubt enter in and cloud my view of the truth and the reality of all that you are, but I can always be free when I choose to be. No one can take that away from me. Even when I make mistakes, your forgiveness can set me free when I simply come to you and admit my failure and ask for your mercy.

Amber thought Saturday would be a difficult day for everyone, but it turned out to be rather nice in many ways. She and Seth met downstairs before breakfast as planned. It had been too wet the last few days to walk down to the creek, so they drove to Wildwood and did their morning devotions in the car. She shared her thoughts from last night with him, and he agreed the hope they had was an amazing gift. They went for a walk onto the bridge spanning the river on the cool and cloudy morning, and the quiet stillness around them reminded her of Grandpa. He had loved the outdoors, the forest, and fishing.

Seth kissed her a little and held her in his arms before they went back to the house, had breakfast with her family, and hung around with everyone until it was time to go into town for the memorial service. It was being held at the church where her grandparents had attended for many years together.

Amber felt overwhelmed by the number of people who came. Her grandfather had been a part of a lot of people's lives, she realized. Of course there was his family: two daughters and two sons and ten grandchildren; those he had attended church with for the fifteen years they had lived here in Sandy, and those he had worked with at the high school and attended church with in their hometown for many years before that.

But there were also many neighbors, those he read to and talked with at the senior center three days a week, those he delivered meals to on a regular basis, and general citizens of the town—doctors, business owners, his barber. It was like every person who had ever known him, even just casually, had been touched deeply enough to come and pay their respects to someone they had considered a neighbor and a friend.

"Charlie was a good man. An honest man. Caring. Sincere. A good friend. A servant. A man after God's own heart." She heard the different words and phrases over and over during the service and from the mouths of others she met and heard talking about her grandpa afterwards.

The graveside service was more private and quiet. Just family and a handful of close friends had been invited. Her grandmother had requested they all sing Grandpa's favorite hymn, and they did before walking away from the site where his body had been laid to rest. A body now free of his eternal soul and the person they all knew.

She and Seth went over to the van and waited with Ben and Hope for her parents and grandmother to return more slowly. While they were standing there, the cousin she was closest to in age and relationship-wise came over to give her a hug and say hello. Mandy was seventeen and also a senior, but she lived in Eugene so Amber didn't get to see her very often.

She thought they sort of looked alike and had heard that many times from her own mother and Mandy's. They had the same hair color and wore it pretty much the same way. Their facial features were similar, and since Mandy had gotten her braces off sometime in the last year, they had matching smiles once again.

But Mandy had blue eyes like Ben. A feature passed down from Grandma's side of the family and also from Mandy's mom. And like her mother, Mandy was petite, about five-two with a slim waist and narrow hips. They had exchanged letters over the past few years, and Mandy had heard about Seth but had never met him. Amber introduced the two of them, and Mandy said a shy hello. She was very quiet and sweet.

They talked until everyone was ready to leave the cemetery and go back to their grandparents' house where everyone was gathering for an afternoon lunch provided by the church.

"Mandy seems nice," Seth commented on the ride back to Sandy. "Are you two the same age?"

"Yes. She's only three months older than me. Her birthday is in May."

"Are you close?"

"Sort of. She lives in Eugene so I don't see her that much, but I always enjoy it when I do. She's very sweet."

"Like someone else I know?"

Amber smiled. "Like you? Yes, I'd say so."

He smiled and kissed her forehead. "It's good to see you smile."

Amber felt sad her grandpa was gone, but she knew everything was going to be all right.

"Mandy worked at a camp this summer," she informed Seth. "Last summer too, actually."

"Where at?"

"At the camp she grew up going to. It's between Eugene and the coast. I don't think it's as big as Laughing Water, about half that size, but it sounds similar from what she's told me."

"Does she know where she's going to college next year?"

"I don't think she's decided yet, but she's smart. Like Colleen smart."

"Maybe you could talk her into going to Lifegate too."

"Maybe," she said, thinking that would be fun. She'd always had a desire to have a closer relationship with her, but only seeing each other twice a year didn't allow for that. Most of her cousins were boys, except for Mandy's older sister,

Melanie, who was twenty-three and had gotten married last year, and one of their younger cousins who was only six.

When they reached her grandparents' house, they went inside and joined the rest of the family, had lunch, and sat around talking about their lives and reminiscing about Grandpa. She talked with Mandy quite a bit more and then when people began to leave around six, Amber learned that Mandy and the rest of her family were planning to spend the night with her grandmother before heading back to Eugene sometime tomorrow.

"You should come spend the night with me," Amber said to her. "Seth has to leave at eight."

"Okay," Mandy said, going to ask her mom if that was all right.

An hour later they were on their way back to the house with Mandy, and they all talked about their respective summers at camp. Amber told Mandy the story about tripping on the way to her cabin during the final week, and the others filled in the parts she had been unconscious for.

Amber hated having to say good-bye to Seth that evening, but having Mandy there helped her to not feel so lonely for him. They went up to her room at nine and got into their pajamas but then stayed up talking for a long time on a more personal level than they'd been able to with everyone else around.

She showed Mandy the scrapbook she'd put together of pictures from camp, and Mandy commented on one of her and Seth standing together in front of the lake, posing for a shot taken near the end of the summer.

"He's so sweet, Amber. I know you told me so in your letters, but I had no idea how much you meant that."

Amber smiled at the picture they were looking at. She liked it because Seth's expression was one-hundred percent him. Happy, genuine, and yes, very sweet.

"Do you think he's the guy you're going to marry?"

"I think he might be," Amber said. "I never imagined I'd be saying that at seventeen, but he's my best friend and everything and more I could ever want in a guy. I really believe God brought us together. I have complete peace about our relationship—most of the time anyway. There are days when I still think, 'No way! He's too good to be true. Okay, when's the bomb going to drop?'"

Mandy laughed.

"How about you? Is there anyone special in your life?"

"No, not yet."

Amber was pretty sure Mandy hadn't dated at all. Last year when she had gone to her sister's wedding, Amber told Mandy about Seth and that she was still in shock because Seth was the only guy she had dated and yet it was going so well. Mandy had told her then she hadn't dated yet either, and unless Mandy simply hadn't mentioned anything in her letters, she knew that was still the case.

"Anyone you have your eye on?" Amber probed further. "Someone at camp, maybe?"

Mandy laughed. "I've got my eyes on plenty, but they don't seem to be looking my way."

"One of these days the right one will. Trust me. If it can happen to me, it can happen to you."

"Really?" Mandy said. "Promise?"

Amber smiled. "I promise, Mandy. You're too sweet to not be a very special part of the right guy's heart."

"But I don't know how to act or what to say whenever a guy I like is around and actually talks to me."

"Just be you, Mandy. That's all I've ever been with Seth. Disasters and messed-up hair and all. But somehow he liked what he saw and made the effort to get to know me. I think that's one of the most special things about him. He looks below the surface, and the right guy will do the same with you. He'll see beyond the shyness and look straight into your heart."

Chapter Nine

By the time Amber and Mandy went to sleep, they had talked about everything from boys, to school, to their plans following graduation, and a lot of little stuff in between. Mandy hadn't decided what college she wanted to go to yet. She felt apprehensive about leaving home and thought she might go to the University of Oregon or a small Christian college that was also in Eugene. She was pretty sure she wanted to become a teacher, and she knew she had the grades to get a good scholarship. Unless she had some major problems with her classes next semester, she would be graduating with straight A's and be one of the valedictorians of her graduating class.

Amber showed her the catalog for Lifegate, and Mandy said she would seriously think about going there. "I've always wished we lived closer to each other," she said. "We can't get much closer than being college roommates."

"I know," Amber replied. "I think being there with you would be so great. You, me, and Kerri rooming together— that would be awesome!"

"Do you think Kerri would like me?"

"Kerri would love you. I know that for a fact. I used to think she was so different from me, but the more I get to know her, the more I see how much alike we are in the things that really matter."

In the morning Mandy went to church with them, and they all went back into town to have lunch with Grandma and Mandy's family. They had to leave at three, and Amber gave Mandy a hug. Her family was planning to come back and stay with Grandma for a few days around Christmas in another two weeks. She had really enjoyed catching up on one another's lives and having the chance to have a conversation with someone who seemed to be on the same spiritual level as herself. It reminded her of the friendships she'd had at camp over the summer.

Amber and her family remained with Grandma for the rest of the day before leaving her alone for the first time since Grandpa had died. Grandma insisted she would be all right, and they all knew she would be with time. She would have sad and lonely times without Grandpa for sure, but her grandmother had learned to depend on God during the difficult times in the past, and she didn't hesitate to remind them all of that.

Amber stayed overnight there twice that week. On Tuesday she had an away basketball game and went over after they returned, and then on Thursday she went there after her home game, finishing up her homework and talking to her grandmother until bedtime.

On Saturday morning she and Ben and Hope drove to a small town south of Eugene for Kyle and Julia's wedding. Seth wasn't able to go with them because this was the weekend of the Christmas play. She missed not having him along but really enjoyed seeing a lot of people from camp, especially Lora. Eric was there too, and Lora seemed happy with him at her side. Lora was also happy for Kyle and Julia whom she had grown up with and were her closest friends along with Eric.

Amber didn't get a chance to talk to Lora in a heart-to-heart way, but she did tell her about her grandfather, and Lora expressed her sympathy and said she would be sure to email her sometime next week. She would be home most of the time while Eric was working and Kyle and Julia were away on their honeymoon.

Amber said she had been praying for her, and Lora said not to stop. "We're still sorting through some things," she said softly.

Amber understood this wasn't a good place to talk about it, and she hoped Lora would write her and share more details if she needed that. And she did intend to keep praying for her. She didn't know why, but she had a really strong feeling Lora and Eric were going to get through this and that God had great things in store for them in the future. She hoped it wasn't just wishful thinking, but if it was, she supposed God knew things she didn't, and either way He would take care of Lora and show her the path He had in mind for her.

On Sunday afternoon Amber helped her mom with getting things ready at the house for the youth Christmas party they were hosting that evening. Most of the feedback had been positive from her friends at church regarding her parents overseeing the youth group now. They were expecting those to come tonight who had been a regular part of their Sunday night Bible study and hoped others would be there too.

As well as eating, playing games, and hanging out, those who came would have a chance to voice their preferences about what they would like to do as a youth group in the future, and her parents were open to doing whatever—within reason, of course.

Seth called her shortly before everyone was scheduled to arrive. He had been busy with running sound and lights for the play this afternoon and needed to get back for their evening performance, but he had a few minutes to give her, and she told him about the wedding and times with her grandmother.

They were both on Winter Break from school this week, and he was planning to come out tomorrow evening after work and stay through the following day. His family was leaving for California on Wednesday and would be gone for a week. But her cousin was returning on Friday and staying through Christmas Day, so she knew that would help keep her from missing Seth too much over Christmas.

"Have fun tonight, sweetheart," he said. "I'll be thinking of you."

"I miss you," she said. "See you tomorrow."

Stacey and Kenny came into the house through the front door after she hung up, so she went to greet them rather than having a good cry about not seeing Seth in over a week. Nicole and Spencer arrived shortly after and were followed by many others, from the sixth graders who had joined their group this fall to some of the high schoolers she hadn't seen much except briefly during the morning church service they attended with their parents. And for the most part the evening went really well from her perspective.

She made an effort to talk to the younger girls she knew by name and face but hadn't connected with yet, and they seemed to open up to her. Initiating conversations had never been her strong point, but after this summer she had become more used to having to do that.

Most of the students left at the scheduled ending time, but Stacey and Kenny hung around along with Nicole and Spencer. Ben and Hope had taken off earlier to go see a movie, but they returned at nine o'clock, and they all sat around talking and playing video games like old times— except Seth wasn't here.

"Can I talk to you for a minute, Ambs?" Stacey whispered in her ear while the boys were heavily focused on their game.

"Sure," she said, rising from the sofa and leading the way out of the living room. Stacey pointed to the stairs like she wanted this to be a completely private conversation, and Amber stepped up to her room with Stacey following behind, closing the door once they were inside.

"What's up, Stace?" She sat on the bed, and Stacey did too before responding.

"Kenny and I had a long talk yesterday, and he's serious about wanting to get married next summer."

"How do you feel about that?"

"I don't know. One minute I'm thinking, 'Okay, yeah. Let's just go for it. Why wait?' And then the next I'm thinking, 'No way! That's completely ridiculous.'"

Amber smiled. "What do you want me to tell you?"

Stacey sighed. "I don't know," she said, flopping sideways onto the bed and burying her face in the blankets.

Amber laughed. "Come on, sit up," she said, slapping her on the behind.

"Ouch!" Stacey said, sitting up and laughing. "That hurt."

"Sorry," she said. "But I'm not listening to this again. What are we supposed to do when we don't know what to do?"

"Bury our head in the sand and hope it goes away?"

"Wrong answer."

"Ask your best friend?"

"Can be helpful, but still not the best thing."

"Pray?"

"You got it!"

"But I've been praying," Stacey wailed. "He's not answering."

"You have to give it time, Stace. He'll answer in His time, not yours, but I promise it will be sometime before next summer."

Amber reached for her Bible and turned to a verse in James she had memorized last spring after they'd had it as a part of their Bible study, but she read it to make sure she said it right.

"If any of you lacks wisdom, he should ask God who gives generously to all without finding fault, and it will be given to him."

"So what am I supposed to pray for? Some kind of a sign?"

"No, ask God for wisdom, and He will give it to you clearly, at the right time and however He chooses. But however He gives it to you, you will know it if you're looking for that and waiting on Him. I know it sounds crazy, but it works! I've done it."

"But what if I don't like the answer?"

"I think you will. God will prepare you for it, and then when it comes you'll be like, 'Of course. It's so obvious that's what is best and what I really want.'"

"You promise?"

"No. God promises."

Stacey took a deep breath and let out a huge sigh. "Okay. Will you pray with me? I'll pray more later too, but I always feel better after you pray."

"You do?"

"Sure. I never hear anybody talk to God the way you do."

Amber took her friend's hand and prayed for her, asking God to give her wisdom about what to do and to give her peace while she waited for the answer. After she finished, she asked her something.

"Do you mind if I ask why Kenny wants to get married next summer?"

"Mostly because he wants to get married while he's going to school on a scholarship and he doesn't have a lot of responsibilities hanging over him. We can have a fun couple of years together before he has to get out in the real world and get a job and everything. He feels like if we wait until he's done with school, then we'll both be so busy, we won't be able to enjoy it."

"What do you think about that?"

"I understand what he's saying, and I think he's right, but I'm not sure I'm ready to get married, you know?"

"Yeah, I know," she said.

They heard a knock on the door, and Stacey thought it might be Kenny coming to see if she was all right, but it turned out to be Ben. He told her she had a phone call, and Amber felt alarmed. It was really late.

"Who is it?"

"Who do you think?"

"But it's so late," she said, knowing he meant it was Seth.

"Yeah, he's such a rebel. You'd better take it before Mom and Dad find out."

She knew he was teasing, but she was seriously concerned. Her guard had gone back up after hearing the news about her grandfather's death when she least expected it. Reaching for the phone, she picked it up and said hello.

"Hi, sweetheart. Sorry to call so late. Did I wake you?"

"No. Stacey and the gang are still here. We were just talking. Is everything okay?"

"Yeah, nothing to worry about. I wanted to ask you something."

"What?"

"How would you like to see me all day tomorrow?"

She smiled. "I'd love it. You don't have to work after all?"

"No. I saw Mr. Davidson at the play tonight, and when I confirmed that I would be there tomorrow, he asked me what the rest of my week looked like, and when I reminded him I would be leaving on Wednesday with my family and he realized I would only be seeing you tomorrow night and Tuesday, he said, 'You're young, Seth. There will be plenty of time to work later. Enjoy extra time with Amber on your break. I don't want to see you until after the first of the year."

"Does that mean I get you next week after you get back?"

"That's what it means, and I'm not wasting any time sleeping-in tomorrow either, so I'll be there by nine."

She laughed. "Okay, I'll be up. What are we doing?"

"I have no idea. I just want to be with you. That's all I care about."

"Okay, I can't wait."

"Me neither. Good night, Amber."

"Good night. I love you."

"I love you more."

"Not possible."

"We'll argue about it tomorrow."

She laughed. "Okay. Bye."

She hung up the phone and looked at Stacey.

"What?"

"Guess what Seth is doing tomorrow?"

"Coming to see you?"

"Yep, and you know why?"

"Why?"

"Because his boss told him he's young and he should spend the time with me instead of working, because they'll be plenty of time to work when he gets older."

"That's pretty cool," Stacey said.

She stared at her.

"What?"

"Did you hear that? An adult—someone who knows what the real world is like—told Seth to spend time with me while he can instead of thinking he'll have more time for that in the future. Gosh, that sounds an awful lot like what Kenny is saying about why he wants to get married before you both finish college and enter the real world."

"Okay, that freaks me out, Amber," she laughed. "Get away from me, you God-seeking guru!"

She laughed and gave her a hug. "Maybe that was a coincidence, but He'll show you, Stacey. He promises that."

Chapter Ten

Amber had a wonderful time with Seth on Monday and Tuesday and felt sad about him leaving, knowing he would be gone for a full week—over Christmas no less, but his sweet kisses and words before he drove away helped her say good-bye without too many tears.

"I have a special surprise planned for you next Saturday after I get back, so keep the day and evening free, okay?"

"Okay," she said.

"And I'll write this week, I promise." He gave her an extra long hug. "I love you, baby."

"I love you too," she whispered.

After he was gone, she went into the house, sat down at the computer to check her email, responded to one from Colleen, and then decided to do some writing. She needed to start thinking about what she would write for her *Creative Writing* final. In addition to an exam, they were also supposed to turn in a final assignment the second week in January that could be on a topic and format of their choice: a descriptive paragraph, poem, short story, or anything else they had learned about this semester, but it would count for one-third of their grade, so she needed to take it seriously.

She wasn't sure what she wanted to do on that yet and decided to work on writing another short story based on the way her parents had met. She'd heard enough of the mushy details over the years and read others from her mother's unfinished novel to get started and was pretty amazed when she had filled several pages of computer screen by the time she felt tired enough to go upstairs and go to bed.

On Wednesday she went Christmas shopping with her mom, and they found most of what they were looking for. She got a nice shirt for Seth and also a frame for a picture of them she planned to give to him. She looked around for something special to get for her grandma but didn't find anything she really liked. After they got home, she thought she might try to write her a poem or something, but she didn't have a definite idea of what she would write about.

After dinner she called Stacey. They both wanted to try and set up a time next week after Seth returned when the four of them could get together, and Stacey said she would talk to Kenny about it and see what times would be good for him. Stacey said she was praying and thinking about how she felt about getting married. At this point she thought waiting one more year to give her time of being away from home and experiencing her relationship with Kenny in a different setting would be good, but she was definitely planning to go to OSU next year. She didn't want to be away from him any longer than necessary.

Stacey shared one more detail that had made her decision more difficult for a few days until she realized something. "Kenny felt like if we were going to get married next year, we should make the decision now so he could apply for married-student housing, but I told him what you said about not worrying about the money—if it's meant to be, I shouldn't have to feel pressured into making a decision based on finances. I could suddenly decide I want to get married in August, and if it was right, God would provide the money for us to live in an apartment.

"I told him the story about how God had already provided the money for you to go to a private college, and that was enough to convince him we don't need to rush anything. So at this point I'm not planning to make a definite decision until at least Spring Break. That would still give me plenty of time to plan a wedding."

"Can I give you one more thing to consider?"

"No," Stacey laughed. "I have enough!"

"Too bad, I'm telling you anyway."

"Okay, what?"

"If you decide to wait another year, I think you and Kenny should apply to be on staff at camp this summer."

"You're so bossy these days! Whatever happened to my quiet friend who never wanted to give her opinion on anything?"

Amber laughed. "Sorry. Jesus has taken over my heart, and He tends to be that way."

"Actually, I've been thinking about that too," Stacey said. "A week at that place changed my life; I can imagine what a whole summer would do. Okay, add that to your prayer list, Princess Amber."

Amber wrote more on her story that night and then checked her email before going to bed. She had been hoping Lora would write to her this week like she'd said, and she was thrilled to see a message waiting for her, but the seriousness of Lora's words made her excitement quickly fade.

Hi, Amber. It was great seeing you at the wedding. Sorry we didn't have much time to talk. It was a busy day for me, and the things I most wanted to say couldn't be said there. To be honest I had decided to break up with Eric this past Sunday. I didn't want to before the wedding, but I've been feeling like I can't go on with trying to make our relationship work. I still love Eric, but since we've been

back together it hasn't felt the same. I've felt frustrated and unhappy a lot, and I'm not usually like that. I've also felt myself guarding my heart rather than giving it completely to Eric like I did before. I thought those feelings would pass with time, but they haven't, so I had decided it wasn't meant to be.

But then on Sunday I had a bad headache and didn't have the chance to talk to him like I wanted to. And on top of that, he was really caring and loving while I wasn't feeling well, and it reminded me so much of the way we once were that now I'm not sure I can really let him go. He's also been saying things lately that are so unlike him. He's been talking about us getting married and being romantic at all hours of the day and taking time off work to be with me instead. It thrills me and scares me to death at the same time! I don't want to get my hopes up that he could actually want to get married sometime soon after graduation, but at the same time I can't help it when he says things like, 'I want to get married in the sunshine on a warm summer day.' Yes, he actually said that! What am I supposed to do, Amber? Help!

So, now I'm feeling unsure again. He's coming back for Christmas, and we'll be having several days together, so maybe I'll be able to talk to him about how I'm feeling and get a more definite idea of where he stands at this point. Don't feel like you have to give me any advice. I'll welcome anything you have to share, but even if all you do is pray for me I'd appreciate it. I think it may have been your prayers that brought Eric back in the first place. And I value your friendship very much. You are wise beyond your years. Keep going with God, sister. You're an inspiration to me.

Love you,
Lora

Amber remembered praying for Lora several times on Sunday. She got chills thinking about it. She went upstairs and wrote out a prayer for Lora and Eric in her journal and then kept writing, interceding on behalf of others on her heart too: Stacey and Kenny, Nicole and Spencer, Ben and Hope, Colleen and Chris, Seth, Kerri, Chad, Matt, friends from camp, her parents, her grandmother, Mandy, Stacey's family, Nicole's parents, kids in the youth group, her teachers and classmates. It was like once she started, she couldn't stop.

"Oh, Jesus. We need you so much," she whispered in the quietness of her room. It was nearly midnight, and she closed her journal and sat there quietly for several minutes. Peace entered her heart that God had heard her prayers and He was in control of all of it.

She couldn't always see the way He was working, but in that moment she knew without a doubt that He was—He had put the desire in her to pray for these people in her life because He cared about them and wanted them to depend on Him and know Him more deeply.

She didn't respond to Lora's email until the following morning, and she didn't give her any advice concerning Eric, but she did let her know she was praying for her and also told her to look up James 1:5, the same verse she had shared with Stacey that talked about asking God for wisdom.

After lunch, she and Ben and her mom went into town to have lunch with Grandma and spend the afternoon with her. Her grandmother was working on a quilt that would be taken to a family in need when she finished it, and her mom sat down to help while she and Ben went down to the basement to sort through some of Grandpa's things. He was a pack-rat, and Grandma said she likely didn't need to hang on to anything that was down there.

"If you see anything you want, you're welcome to have it," she told them. "And anything that's in nice shape and you think someone might want, put it all together in one place and we can donate it to charity. But anything that looks like garbage, don't be afraid to toss it. I loved him dearly, but he had a terrible time throwing anything away."

Amber had to smile. She knew her grandparents had loved each other very much, but they obviously didn't always agree over every little thing. They were two people with different interests and ambitions. And yet their love for each other had made it work for over fifty years.

So far she and Seth hadn't discovered anything about one another that made them incompatible, but she knew they were different in some ways. Seth was a morning person, and she was a nite-owl. Seth was neat and organized, she was like her grandpa, cluttering up her small room with all kinds of things and then never wanting to throw anything away. Seth thrived on leadership and being up front in a crowd. She would rather follow the lead of others and work behind the scenes.

It was cold in the basement, but once they started working, Amber warmed up, and going through her grandfather's things was bittersweet. Little things reminded her of him: stacks of old magazines and newspaper articles; He was always reading something. Old lamps and small appliances and broken clocks he hadn't got around to fixing or had kept for the parts to fix something else. Lots of old books—history and geography textbooks from the 1970s to modern day ones. Atlases galore. She decided to keep a few of those for herself that were in nice shape. She also put some classic novels in her stack along with an old phonograph that she doubted worked, but it had a quaint appeal she thought might have decorative use in the future.

Ben kept a lot of Grandpa's tools and some books and old magazines. Ben had started out in Elementary Education but had a love for history and geography too, and he was now looking to become a middle school teacher specializing in those areas. Grandma had already told Ben he could have Grandpa's most prized atlases he kept upstairs along with other history books Ben would likely find useful.

They had sorted a lot into the two piles, one for charity and another for the dumpster by the time her mom needed to get home to make dinner, but Amber knew they would need to come back several more times to weed through everything. Before they left, her grandmother pointed out boxes in her closet that contained something she thought might interest her. They were heavy, and Ben pulled them out and set them by the door. Amber opened the top one and saw stacks and stacks of notebooks.

"Those are your grandpa's travel journals," she said. "Every time we went someplace, he wrote down everything we saw and did. Sometimes he used them for reference later when he was teaching about a particular city or area, but mostly they've sat untouched. One time I asked him why he kept them all, and he said they might be of use to someone someday. And when you read that story, I thought maybe you could use them to help you write about places you've never been to. If you don't want them, don't feel like you have to take them, but I wanted to let you know they're here and you're welcome to them."

Amber didn't hesitate to respond. "I'd love to have them. Thank you," she said, giving her grandmother a hug. She did think she might be able to use them to help her write, if she ended up doing more beyond this semester, but she also wanted them as a keepsake-memory of her grandfather. Of all of her grandpa's loves, traveling was at the top of the list.

This would be a special way to always have him with her. She could read what he had written and imagine she was seeing it all too.

"Are Uncle Tom and Aunt Beth still coming tomorrow?" she asked as Ben started carrying the boxes out to the van.

"Yes. They should be here by mid-afternoon, I expect. You're welcome to come here and sleep in that room with Mandy some of the time if you want."

"Tell her I'll be here—tomorrow night!" she said, not trying to hide her excitement.

On the way home Ben said he thought it would be fun for her and Mandy, along with himself and their cousin T.J., who was Ben's age, to do something together on Saturday. Amber thought that would be fun too, and she could hardly wait until tomorrow evening to see Mandy again. There had been something very special about the time they'd spent together two weeks ago, and she wanted more. It reminded her of when she had first started dating Seth, and the time with him was so uplifting and special she felt like she couldn't get enough.

But while she waited for tomorrow to come, she had plenty to keep her busy that evening and into the following day. She had taken out one of her grandpa's journals, just to see what they were like, and it captivated her right from the start. Her grandmother had been right when she said he wrote about *everything* they did and saw. His descriptions of the places they had visited were very detailed and descriptive—as if she was right there seeing it all too.

And he didn't just write about the places he had visited, but also about the one he had seen them with. Things his beloved wife said and did at each place were included in the narrative, and his love for her came shining through. At the end of his entry dated July 4th, he wrote:

Another perfect Fourth of July with my sweet Dorothy. No matter where we see the fireworks together each year—in our hometown or above the beautiful waters of Puget Sound, one thing remains the same: My love for her keeps right on growing, and there's no place I'd rather be than by her side.

Chapter Eleven

Dear Amber,

Have I told you lately that I love you? How you completely make my day and keep my heart warm? It's only been two hours since I've seen you, but I'm already missing your soft touch and sweet kisses. I will miss you this week, very much.

I was thinking on the drive home that if we both end up going back to camp next summer and to college together next year, we'll only have about five more months of spending time apart before we can see each other every day again—possibly for the rest of our lives. Does that interest you at all? Do you feel as thrilled at the prospect as I do? Oh, sweetheart, I can't wait. I'll be counting the days (172 to be exact).

I hope you're having a good week with your family. It's probably Thursday by now for you. You should get another letter from me on Saturday, and I'll email you on Christmas day—and probably call you too. And then I'll be back on Wednesday, holding you in my arms and wishing it never has to end.

I think I might be in love with you. I hope I have you forever.

> *Missing you baby,*
> *Seth*

After she had returned from camp, Amber had gone through all of Seth's letters he had ever sent to her, including the emails she had printed out that were extra special, and sorted them into two categories: those that were more generic and informative, and those she absolutely loved. This one was definitely going into the shoebox where the more special ones were kept.

Turning off her light with a warm feeling in her heart, she asked God to keep Seth and his family safe on their trip and to return him to her alive and well next week. Over the last few days she had often thought of her grandmother having to go on without Grandpa, never to see him again until she joined him in Heaven, and it had made her see a week without Seth as just that: a week. She could handle that.

In the morning she decided to wrap her Christmas presents and then went downstairs to finish writing her story. She read through the whole thing and made some changes and tried to decide if she should use it as her writing final assignment or come up with something else.

She thought about it over lunch and read more of Grandpa's journals. If she read them enough, she thought they might inspire a story, and even if they didn't, she did enjoy reading her grandfather's words.

Grandma called at two o'clock. Her dad was at work and her mom was painting, so she answered the phone and talked to her for a few minutes. Her aunt and uncle hadn't arrived yet, but her grandmother expected them at any time, and she invited her family to come for dinner tonight. Supposing that would be fine, Amber accepted the invitation and then went to tell her mom about it.

"Is it all right if I stay over at Grandma's tonight with Mandy?" she asked after her mom had said they could go.

"Sure, sweetie. That's fine."

"Did I tell you I talked to her about going to Lifegate next year?"

"No. Is she interested?"

"Yes. She hasn't decided where she wants to go and thinks it might be a possibility."

"That would be fun," her mom said. "Would that mean you wouldn't room with Kerri then?"

"No, the girls' dorm rooms there hold four people. They're actually like little suites with a sleeping and study area for two people on each side and a bathroom in between."

"That sounds nice. Do you think you all might try and go visit the campus sometime?"

"Seth and Kerri are stopping by on their way back next week. There won't be anyone there, so they won't be able to see inside the buildings and everything, but they can see where it's at and if the campus matches what the pictures show."

"Well, your dad and I want you to know that if you want to go visit sometime this spring before you make your final decision, that would be fine."

"You mean without you guys? Just me and Seth and Kerri?"

"Yes."

Amber didn't know why that shocked her, but it did. "Wow. I guess you really do trust Seth, don't you."

"Yes, and we trust you too, Ammie."

Amber stepped over to her mother and gave her a hug. "Thanks for teaching me what's right, and for praying. My relationship with Seth is so special, and I wouldn't want it any other way."

"Neither would I," she said. "And I promise the blessings don't stop now. They'll be with you for the rest of your life—just like they were for Grandma and Grandpa and like they are for me and your dad. God knows what He's talking about. Don't stop listening, okay?"

She smiled. "I won't. And I'm pretty sure Seth won't either."

***

Stepping into her grandmother's house at five-thirty, Amber could hear that her relatives had arrived. They were all in the living room, talking with Grandma, and she was happy to see that in addition to Mandy and T.J., her other cousin, Melanie, and her husband, Kevin, had come too. Melanie had been here for the memorial service, but Kevin hadn't because he had to work. This was the first time she'd seen them together since they had gotten married last year, and she wasn't quite sure why, but seeing them together, still appearing happy and in love, gave her a very warm feeling.

She greeted everyone with heartfelt hugs but hung on to Mandy a little more tightly. After a lively dinner with Uncle Tom sitting at the head of the table rather than her grandpa, several of them played a game of *Clue* and then she and Mandy went back to the bedroom they would be sharing for tonight.

Mandy told her she was seriously thinking of going to Lifegate, and Amber was thrilled. She had tried to not get her hopes up and wasn't expecting Mandy to say anything about it this soon, but Mandy had talked to her mom and dad, and they were supportive. She had also been praying and didn't feel God telling her 'no' at this point. Mandy would be considering all her options in the coming months, but she was definitely open to the possibility and seemed as excited at the prospect as she was.

After getting into their pajamas, they talked late into the night, and Amber told her more about Seth at Mandy's request. Mandy asked how she had known he was the guy for her, and Amber started at the beginning, sharing significant events and times they'd had together that had given her strong feelings for him quickly but also kept their relationship grounded and based on the right things.

"I think one of the biggest things was his words matched his actions. He would tell me things, either in letters or face-to-face, and then he showed me he meant what he said."

"Like what?" Mandy asked.

"Like telling me he missed me and enjoyed spending time with me and then making the effort to see me as much as possible, even when it wasn't convenient for him and he had to drive an hour each way. Saying he cared about me and I was special to him and then always making me feel that way too. And telling me he was committed to keeping our relationship pure and giving me a True-Love-Waits bracelet and then actually keeping his kisses under control and his hands where they should be."

Mandy was quiet for a moment and then said, "You know, Amber. After we talked last time, I went back home and thought seriously about the different guys I like—or at least think I do—and I realized several of them wouldn't make good dating-material. And the few I think might be okay, I actually don't know very well. I see them at church and school, but I honestly have no idea what they would be like on a date."

"I know what you mean," she said. "I was the same way. It's honestly a miracle none of the guys I thought would be so perfect ever asked me out. I look at most of them now and think 'What did I ever see in them?' And I'm so thankful God protected me from getting caught up with any of them and brought me Seth at just the right time."

"Did you know he was different, even before you went out with him?"

"I think I did. I didn't realize it so much at the time, but he was an absolute sweetheart right from the beginning—even when I first met him at Taco Bell and he didn't even know me. And every time I saw him that week, he was the exact same way and always made me feel relaxed and comfortable, like I could just be myself."

"So you think God will answer my prayers for my Seth to come along one of these days?"

"Yes, Mandy. And he will be so great you'll keep saying over and over, 'I can't believe it! How did I ever get this guy?'"

Mandy laughed. She was quiet for a moment and then said, "You know something, Amber?"

"What?"

"You're an answer to prayer."

"I am?"

"Yes. My first summer at camp I had a lot of fun, and I grew some spiritually, but then I went back home and fell back into the same lazy habits of not reading my Bible and stuff. And then this summer I formed several close friendships and we sort of pushed each other to really get serious about our faith, and at the end of the summer I didn't want to go home because I knew there wasn't anybody like that in my youth group or at school—at least not that I knew of, and I was afraid of losing all the ground I'd gained over the summer.

"And so I started praying I would find someone who was either on the same level as me spiritually or was even stronger, but since I've been back I haven't really connected with anyone like that. I've been doing okay though. I think God wanted me to look to Him instead of other people, but I was beginning to lose heart and think I was a total freak for wanting to grow in my faith, you know?"

"Yes. I know. That's another thing about Seth. We both had the same serious desire to get to know Jesus better, and he's kept me on track like nobody else ever has."

"You haven't been with me these last two weeks, but just knowing I'm not the only one, and hearing about all the great stuff God is doing in your life has helped me to keep pressing on. My devotions these last two weeks have been better than they've been for several weeks, and I couldn't wait to see you again today."

"We should start writing each other once a week. You tell me what you've been learning about God, how you've seen Him at work in your life, and anything you want me to pray about, and I'll do the same, okay?"

"Okay. I'd really like that."

"Me too."

On Saturday they hung around the house in the morning. Ben came into town after lunch, and she and Mandy along with T.J., Ben, Melanie, and Kevin went shopping—well, she and Mandy and Melanie went shopping while Ben and T.J. and Kevin went to the nearby video arcade and then they met back up to go see a movie and had pizza for dinner.

That night Mandy came over to her house and went to church with her in the morning. Mandy's family along with Grandma came out for lunch at their house and spent the rest of the day with them. They all went to the Christmas Eve service and then caroling together afterwards, along with about ten other kids from the youth group before Amber had to say good-bye to Mandy.

She would be seeing her for a little while tomorrow before her family headed back to Eugene, but Amber knew it wouldn't be as special as the past two days had been.

"Think seriously about Lifegate, you hear me?"

"I will," Mandy said. "Although, I'm not sure it will take much. I think Jesus is making Himself pretty clear."

Chapter Twelve

On Christmas morning Amber woke up feeling content and happy. This had been a long and busy month. The Winter Dance seemed like a long time ago. Her grandfather's passing was fresher in her mind, but slowly she had accepted it as a reality and knew life would go on as before in many ways. She'd had a fun time with Mandy over the weekend, and she would be seeing Seth in another two days. And she had Christmas presents waiting for her downstairs.

The thought made her spring out of bed and hurry down to the living room in her pajamas. Her parents had always placed one unwrapped gift for her and one for Ben in front of the tree early Christmas morning. Many times over the years she had known what to expect. She had her grand list and knew which one would most likely be set apart from the others, but this year she honestly had no clue. Other than a few Christian music albums and books she had mentioned wanting, along with her usual request for new clothes, she hadn't given her parents any solid ideas.

No one else was downstairs when she arrived. Stepping toward the tree tucked in the corner of the living room, she saw two items in front and wasn't sure which one was for her. There was a new camera and a laptop. She already had a camera that was pretty new, and Ben already had a computer her parents had gotten him for graduation, but she couldn't believe her parents would be getting her one now instead of waiting until she was closer to going to college.

"Are you surprised?" she heard a voice behind her say. Turning around, she saw Ben coming into the room.

"Is that for me?" she asked, pointing to the laptop.

"I already have one, and I asked for a new camera, so I guess so."

She felt shocked and asked Ben why they would be getting her one now instead of waiting until she went to college.

"They thought you could use this one up in your room and wherever you want to write your stories instead of being stuck in that corner with distractions all around you."

She hadn't thought of that and knew it would be cool to write upstairs or at the library during her free period or down at her favorite spot by the creek once warmer weather came. She could also take it to camp this summer.

"Did you give them the idea?" she asked.

"They asked me for advice on what kind to get you, but it was their idea. They think you write really well and would love to see you pursue it seriously. Me too."

"Really?"

"Yes, really. Didn't that boyfriend of yours tell you how great that story was you wrote about Grandma and Grandpa?"

"Yes, but he's a little biased."

"That may be true, but he's not the only one who thinks so."

Ben picked it up off the floor and set it on the coffee table, turning it on and showing her how it worked. She wasn't an expert on computers and was glad to see it didn't seem too complicated to use.

When her parents came downstairs, she thanked them sincerely and heard their similar comments about thinking she could use it to do more writing. They all began opening their gifts from one another, and Amber realized this was the last Christmas they would share together before she was in college too. Her senior year was almost halfway over, and while in some ways she couldn't wait for graduation, in other ways five months seemed like a very short amount of time.

Seth called as they were finishing up their gift exchange. Taking the call, she heard his sweet voice and began walking toward the stairs for a little privacy but didn't go all the way up to her room.

"How's your morning been so far?" he asked.

"Good," she replied, sitting on the steps. "I got a laptop."

"Sweet. I hoped they would decide to go with that."

"You knew about it?"

"They asked me if I thought you would like one, and I said I thought so. I like having the freedom to take mine anywhere, especially when I'm writing something."

"I can't believe my parents are asking you for advice on what to get me for Christmas. It's like—that's crazy, Seth!"

"I know. It's pretty wild. I think they know this thing between us isn't going away."

"Thanks for whatever you said. They obviously listened, and I'm excited to see what I end up doing with it."

"Don't be afraid to go for it, sweetheart. I think God has a lot more in mind for you than a few writing assignments."

Amber felt a chill pass through her when he said that. She had been thinking of a story idea last night before she went to bed. The Christmas caroling had inspired it. She pictured a scene with a shy girl like Mandy catching a nice boy's eye in her youth group as they walked a neighborhood street, singing songs and trying to keep warm. She wasn't sure what the story was about yet, but it was enough to get her started.

Seth asked about her week, and she told him about her grandpa's journals and her time with Mandy. He was having an okay time there, but he was missing her. She often felt she missed him more than he missed her, simply because he tended to be very busy during the week. But his cousins were all older than him, most of them married with kids, so other than Kerri and Micah, he didn't have anyone to talk to or much to do.

"You need me or something?" she teased.

"I'm aching for you right now, baby. Honestly, you better have one great hug waiting for me and lots of kisses because I'm going on empty here."

"We can fit a lot of those into six days."

"I know. I can't wait. I'll be there early on Wednesday morning."

"I'll be up."

They talked for a little while longer before he had to go. They were staying with his grandparents but going to another relative's house for a big Christmas lunch. She and her family were going to Aunt Dawn's house for a family get-together too, so she needed to take a shower and get ready.

"I'm counting the hours," he said. "Only forty-six more to go."

"Are you going to tell me what my surprise for Saturday is?"

"Yes. On Saturday."

She laughed.

"You still think I'm funny?"

"You always make me laugh, even when you're being a pest."

"And you always make me smile, even when I can't see you."

"You're going to be seeing a lot more of me in five months."

"I know. I can't wait."

"You get a preview this week."

"Speaking of this week," he said. "My parents were thinking of having your parents over to our house on New Year's Eve. They could drive in with us in the afternoon and stay until we go to the youth group party, or later if they want. Do you think they might want to do that?"

"I'll ask," she said. "Would it just be them, or are your parents having a bunch of people over?"

"No, it would be just them. And our normal full house, of course."

She laughed. "Okay. I'll let you know."

"My dad's giving me the look now. I'd better go."

"Okay. Bye. I love you."

"I love you too, sweetheart. See you."

She went to ask her parents about New Year's Eve, and they said they could probably do that. Then she went upstairs and took a shower. Deciding to wear the new dress her mom and dad had given her, she slipped on the velvet-like fabric that hung simply on her shoulders and fell just above her knees. It was a simple but festive-looking dress, and she was a little surprised by how great it looked on her. Sort of elegant. Maybe too much for an afternoon with family, but when she saw her mom dressed up in one of her fancier outfits also, she decided it was all right.

"I really like your hair that way," her mom said after she commented on the dress looking nice on her. "Is that the way you wore it for the dance?"

"Yes, eventually," she laughed.

"I hear a story in that."

"Kerri straightened it for me, and it was fine at first, but then it started bugging me a little. I kept brushing it out of my eyes, and Seth finally said, 'You should pull it back or something,' but I didn't have anything with me. So when I was in the bathroom with Erin, waiting for Kerri to arrive, she took one of her hair clips out and gave it to me, and then after the whole thing with Pete was over and we had gone back into the ballroom, Seth reminded me how much he always liked it this way."

She had worn it with the sides pulled back into a clip one of the evenings during the week at camp when they had first met, and Seth had told her how much he liked it a few weeks later when she wore it that way for church. After that she had worn it back a lot more until she got her hair cut later in the fall and the sides were too short for it to work.

Eventually her hair had grown out, but while they were at camp this summer, she almost always had it in a ponytail except for sometimes on Saturdays when she would wear it loose. She had forgotten how much Seth liked it pulled back until the night of the dance, and since then she had been doing so almost every time they were together.

When she saw him on Wednesday morning, that's the way she wore it, and the first words out of his mouth were: "You're driving me crazy with that look."

"That's the idea," she replied, receiving a breathtaking kiss. He had missed her.

He had something in his hand to show her. "This was waiting in the mail for us when we got home last night," he said.

He flipped over the envelope, and she saw the Compassion name and logo in the upper left corner. "A letter from Jonathan," he said, referring to the little boy from

Columbia they had signed up to sponsor at the concert. They had received his picture and information about him then, and they had written a letter to him right away, but this was the first one they had received in return.

Amber smiled, and she could see that Seth hadn't opened it yet so they could read it together. Going to sit on the porch swing, Seth took it out of the envelope as she sat beside him. He began reading the letter aloud that had been translated from Spanish to English.

"Dear Seth and Amber,

I greet you affectionately in the name of our Lord Jesus Christ. My name is Janeth, and I am Jonathan's mother. He is learning to write, so I am writing to you on his behalf for now. When he gets older he wants to write to you himself. He wants to say thank you for being his sponsors. He was so excited when the center told him about you. He wants to know all about you and your families and wonders if you have any pets. He prays for you every night before he goes to sleep, and he hopes that God will bless you very much.

Jonathan likes to play soccer and play with toy cars. They have some at the center where he is learning about Jesus. He has three older siblings who have been going to the center, and he is excited he gets to go now too. He would like to have a picture of you and hopes you can write to him soon.

God bless you,
Janeth"

Amber had a warm feeling in her heart, and she knew Seth must too. Lifting her eyes from the letter, she kissed him on the cheek and said, "Thanks for having us do this. I got money from my grandma for Christmas, and I want to use some of it to send to Jonathan this month, okay?"

"You mean since I haven't been working much?" he laughed.

"Yes, and since I know you probably spent what you did make on Christmas presents for me."

He didn't deny it. She had no idea what to expect from him this year. Last year he'd been sweet and romantic, giving her the teddy bear and little trinkets and the silver ring she had on today. Since he had already given her a necklace for the dance, she hoped he remembered that was supposed to be part of her Christmas gift and hadn't gotten her another expensive gift since then.

They went inside. Her mom was home, but her dad was at work, and Ben left at ten-thirty to go pick up Hope. They were going snowboarding today and had invited them to come along, but both she and Seth wanted to relax and just be together today. Tomorrow they were planning to spend the afternoon and evening with Stacey and Kenny, and on Friday Chris was coming out to see Colleen and they had talked about maybe going up to the mountain with them.

Seth and his family had stopped by the Lifegate campus yesterday on their way back, and he told her and her mom all about it, saying it was even more beautiful than the pictures and a lot bigger than he was expecting.

"I think you're going to like it," he said.

She hadn't told him what her mom had said about it being okay for them to go see the campus together sometime, so she did, and Seth said his parents were willing to drive them down another time when she could come too. But hearing

118

Seth's comments and impressions was enough for her to know they had likely found the college for them.

After lunch Amber went upstairs and got her computer and brought it down to show Seth. He asked if she had used it to write anything yet, and she told him she had but didn't give him any specifics. She had started her story about the girl who liked a boy in her youth group and what happened between them when they went Christmas caroling, but she wasn't sure where she was going with it or how long it would end up being. She thought she might like to try and write a whole novel rather than a short story, but she had no idea if she could do such a thing or what Seth would think of her lofty notions, so she kept that to herself.

She suggested they open their gifts now. Her mom had gone out to her painting studio, so they had some privacy, and she was glad when he agreed instead of saying she had to wait until later. They were planning to go out to dinner this evening, and she thought he might want to wait until then, but she thought they had already waited long enough.

He went out to his car to get the gifts he had for her, and she pulled his from under the tree and sat in the middle of the living room to wait for him to return. The phone rang when she heard Seth come in through the front door, and she went to answer it.

"Hello," she said cheerily.

"Hi, is this Amber?"

"Yes."

"Hi, Amber. This is Loralyn."

"Lora! Hey, how are you?"

"Good. Very good in fact."

Amber felt a smile form on her face and had the feeling Lora had something very special to tell her. She'd never called her before. They always just emailed or wrote letters.

"What's up?" she asked.

"Well, last night I had planned to talk to Eric about what he was thinking concerning our future. I had decided I needed to be completely honest with him about everything and say if he was having any doubts about our relationship I didn't think I could keep hanging on."

"What did he say?"

Lora laughed. "The day I figure out how a guy's mind works is the day the sun stops shining."

Seth had set his gifts on the floor beside where she had placed hers and then walked over to her standing by the dining room table. She looked up at him, and he slipped his arms around her waist as Lora shared her happy news.

"He asked me to marry him, Amber."

Amber gasped. "He did?"

"Yes. And I was so not expecting it."

"Did he have a ring and everything?"

"Yes, and I asked him if he was sure, and he said he's been planning this since October. I about fainted!"

Amber laughed but had tears glistening in her eyes. She leaned into Seth and expressed her genuine happiness. "Oh, Lora. That's so great. I couldn't stop praying."

"Thanks, Amber. I know it made a difference."

Chapter Thirteen

Lora couldn't talk long, but she had wanted to call and share that. Amber told her she was glad and happy about the news. Other than Seth's arrival this morning, she didn't think anything could be a better Christmas gift.

After she hung up, she turned in Seth's arms and held him tightly for several moments. "They're engaged, Seth," she said, feeling incredibly happy for them.

"So I guessed," he said.

She leaned back and looked into Seth's eyes. "Do you remember when you told me this summer I should pray for Eric to realize he doesn't need to plan and figure everything out on his own but to trust God to guide him?"

"Yes."

"That's one of the main things I've prayed for in all of this, and Lora said when he asked her and she questioned if this is what he really wants, he said he didn't want to try and figure out the future but concentrate on them and their relationship and let God take care of the rest."

"I guess God heard you."

"Yes, but I never would have thought to pray for that if you hadn't told me to."

He smiled and sat on one of the stools along the counter so he was at eye-level with her. "We're a team, baby."

She melted into his sweet kisses, and she felt an emotional connection passing between them she hadn't experienced before. She felt like his partner—like he couldn't do certain things without her, and she couldn't know and serve God completely without him.

In that moment she truly believed they were going to be together for the rest of their lives. She didn't know when they were going to get married, maybe not for several more years, maybe not until they graduated from college, but she knew it was going to happen. It wasn't wishful thinking and romantic dreams; it was the reality that God had brought them together for a specific purpose.

She didn't know if Seth felt it too, but after several enjoyable kisses, he did hold her in his arms, magnifying the feeling in her heart all the more.

Eventually they got around to opening their gifts, and he seemed to like the choices she had made. They were all things he had given her ideas on except for one. She had gotten him a nice shirt, similar to the one he had on now, except it was a different color.

"Do you like it?" she asked. "You can take it back if you don't. I just thought of you when I saw it."

"I like it," he said, leaning over to kiss her sweetly. "And every time I wear it, I'll think of you."

She could tell he was being honest with her, and she felt a little better about giving him clothes when she opened his next gift and saw he had given her something to wear too—in her hair, and she never would have guessed he would have gotten her such a thing.

There were three of them. Clips like the ones she used to keep her hair back like it was now, only these were much more beautiful than the basic ones she had. One was made with a bunch of tiny pearls, another was silver with little raised hearts all over the surface, and the third was gold with blue stones weaved into a braided pattern across the center.

"If you don't like them you can't take them back because I got them at a little shop in California."

She laughed. "Like I would anyway. They're beautiful." She took the plain clip she currently had in her hair and replaced it with the silver one and then turned to the side to model it for him.

"I really like your hair that way," he said. "I don't know why, but it does something to me."

She smiled at him. "Yeah, that kind of shirt on you does the same thing to me."

She handed him the wrapped box with the picture she had put into a frame. He opened it and took the frame out, staring at the photograph for a long time. When he looked at her, he had tears in his eyes.

"I had the same reaction when I first saw it," she said, moving over to lean against his side and look at the picture too. It had been taken at camp this summer without either of them knowing it—the day Seth had prayed for her at the campfire area before her full week of counseling.

"Who took this?"

"Lora. She sent it to me after the summer. She had been walking around that day, taking pictures on one of her walks, and she stopped by the campfire area to pray, and we were there, so she took our picture."

He put his arm around her waist, holding her gently against him. "You're wearing your hair that way," he said.

"I know. Isn't that wild? I hardly ever wore it that way this summer. I didn't even think about that until I wrapped this the other night. And look, you're wearing the camp t-shirt I gave you."

He was quiet for a moment and then spoke. "When we visited Lifegate yesterday, from the moment we turned onto the road leading to the campus and as we walked along the pathways between the buildings, I kept imagining you there by my side, and I had the exact same feeling I had when we prayed together at camp that day."

"What kind of feeling?"

"Like this is what we're meant to do—be in ministry together."

She admitted her earlier thoughts. "I had that same feeling when we were talking about Eric and Lora and you said that to me about us being a team."

"I think God might be calling me to be a youth pastor, Amber."

"That doesn't surprise me, Seth."

"It scares me."

She didn't say anything. It scared her a little too, but mostly she felt excited about whatever lay ahead for them in the future.

"Will you be by my side if God leads me that way?"

"As long as you'll have me."

'That's going to be a long time."

"I know."

Seth sighed. He was silent for a long moment, and she glanced up at him and saw his eyes were closed. She remained quiet. He finished his silent prayer with words for her ears also.

"You lead, Jesus. We'll follow."

He held her for another few minutes and then handed her the last gift. She took it from him. It appeared to be a book, and she was right. It was rather thick, and she was very surprised when she saw the title: *How To Write A Novel.*

"Seth!" She laughed. "Are you insane? I write one good short story, and you think I can write a novel?"

"No, I don't know that for certain, but I'd love to see you try. Have you ever thought about it?"

She didn't respond. He wasn't supposed to ask her that.

"You have?"

"Yes."

"Maybe this will help you get started."

"I already did," she said, burying her face in her hands.

He took her into his arms and laughed softly. "Just go for it and see what happens."

They decided to go for a walk after picking up all the paper and putting away their gifts, stopping by her mom's studio to let her know where they would be and then heading down the driveway. It had been raining and snowing off and on for several days, but today was dry.

"I want to ask you something, Amber, and I want you to be completely honest with me, okay?"

"Okay," she replied.

"Promise?"

"I promise."

"Were you expecting me to get you a ring?"

She wasn't sure what he meant. "A ring? You mean like you did last year?"

He stopped walking and turned to face her. She looked up at him, and he reached for her left hand.

"No, I mean for this finger," he said, holding it gently in the space between them.

"An engagement ring?"

"Yes."

She smiled. "No, I wasn't, Seth. Honest."

He didn't respond.

Her heart started pounding. "Why? Do you have one?"

"No," he said. "I thought maybe because of what I said this summer, and with Kenny asking Stacey, that you would be expecting me to do the same."

"No, I wasn't," she said. "I don't feel ready for that. I won't even be eighteen until the end of the summer, and I don't feel like we need to rush into it right out of high school. I'm very happy to keep on being your girlfriend."

"I'm happy with the way things are too," he said. "I thought about it and even prayed about it, but I don't feel like it's the right time."

She leaned into him and laid her head on his chest. He held her gently.

"When I ask you to marry me, I don't want it to be a surprise," he said. "I mean, maybe it will be a surprise in that moment—like you weren't expecting me to ask right then, but I don't want a proposal to come as a total shock because I hadn't already let you know how strongly I feel about you by that point."

She laughed and looked into his eyes.

"What?"

"I don't think I would have been too shocked if you would have asked me today."

"And what would you have said?"

She thought about that and replied honestly. "I think I would have said what I just told you, but I also would have agreed to pray about it."

The next two days were relaxing and fun. Their time with Stacey and Kenny on Thursday seemed more special than usual. Kenny had always been sweet and caring toward Stacey, but after being away at school for three months, he had matured a lot, and he didn't just treat her well but like she was the most special thing in the world to him. And that made sense if Kenny had asked her to marry him.

On Friday Chris and Colleen were supposed to come out, but Colleen called her before lunch and said Chris had to work unexpectedly. Colleen sounded a little upset, and Amber could understand if Chris had called her to say he wasn't coming today, but something told her it might be more than that, so she asked.

"Is everything okay, Colleen?"

When Colleen answered, her words came out shaky, and she sounded on the brink of tears. "Not really. I saw him on Christmas Eve, and he seemed sort of distant, and now I feel like he's avoiding me, but I have no idea why."

Chapter Fourteen

Colleen remained on Amber's mind for the rest of the day. She tried calling her on Saturday morning, and again before she and Seth went into town to visit her grandmother in the afternoon, but she only got her voice mail.

Colleen didn't have anything concrete to go on to know for certain there was a problem. Chris hadn't said anything to her directly, but Amber agreed it did seem strange he had canceled on her twice in the same week, especially since neither of them were in school right now.

Her grandmother's stories helped Amber get her mind off of it. She was also curious to know what big surprise Seth had planned for her this evening. All she knew was they needed to be back at the house in time to change into something nice, and because of the time Seth had told her they needed to be ready, she assumed they were going to dinner, but she supposed Seth had more planned than that.

At five o'clock she walked down the stairs dressed in the long blue skirt she had gotten for her birthday last year. She had chosen it because it had been the first dress Seth had ever seen her wear, and because he always told her she looked nice whenever she wore it.

He met her at the bottom of the stairs and said what she expected. "You look beautiful, sweetheart."

"Thank you," she said, taking in his attire. He was wearing his best slacks and a dressy shirt with a tie. "You look rather fine yourself."

He kissed her sweetly and then her dad interrupted them. He was dressed up and wearing a tie too.

"All right, Seth," he said. "Let me by to go see if my girl is ready yet."

They stepped out of his way, and Amber turned back to Seth. "My parents are going?"

He took her hand and walked toward the living room. "Yes. This is definitely a group date."

She had no idea what he had planned and didn't bother to try and guess. Stepping into the living room, she saw her brother relaxing on the couch, and he was dressed up too. The only time she had ever seen Ben wear a tie had been at his high school graduation.

"Benjamin Wilson! What are you wearing?"

He flashed her a crooked smile. "Seth said to wear a tie, so I am."

"So, this is going to be you and me, my mom and dad, and Ben and Hope?"

Seth didn't answer. Her mom and dad joined them moments later, and Seth said it was time to go. They all headed for the door, and when she stepped outside ahead of Seth, she gasped. There was a black limousine sitting in their driveway.

"Surprise," Seth said softly in her ear.

She looked around and no one else seemed surprised by the limo's presence. "Am I the only one who has no idea what's going on?"

"No. The other girls are clueless too."

"What other girls?"

The back door of the limo opened and Kenny, Chris, and Spencer emerged. They were dressed in their finest also.

"We're picking up Hope, Stacey, Colleen, and Nicole on the way. They don't know any more than you do."

"Did you arrange all this?"

He smiled. "I thought you were entitled to a less crazy night than we had for the winter dance."

They all piled into the limo and stopped to pick up each of the guy's dates on the way. But the surprises didn't end there. When they arrived at their destination, Amber had no idea where they were. Going inside the nice restaurant, she could see it was a fancy place complete with a grand piano someone was playing beautifully and a dance floor in front of the large, picturesque windows overlooking the Columbia River.

They were seated at two large round tables. She enjoyed having everyone together, but she thought Seth inviting her parents to join them was a special touch. After they had ordered their food, Seth asked her to dance, and they did. Everyone else followed their lead, and having her friends surrounding them, enjoying the music and each other, Amber realized she had been praying for every one of them—as individuals and couples. She felt overwhelmed by everything God had done in her life and those she cared about.

"This is so special, Seth. Thank you."

"I have something for you," he said, taking a folded piece of paper out of his pocket. "I wrote this last night. Do you want to hear it?"

"Of course."

He read it to her softly but over the sound of the delicate piano music. She laid her head on his shoulder and listened.

"We're dancing here, in this place
I love the smile that's on your face
The music is sweet and so is the beat
Of my heart that's in love with you

I hope you won't forget this night
The times we danced and I held you tight
And I hope and pray our life together
Will be a dance to remember

A dance of joy, a dance of love
A dance of honesty, a dance from above
You've captured my heart, so please don't let go
I love you, Amber; I love you so."

She smiled. "I never get tired of hearing that."

"That I love you?"

"Yes."

He kissed her sweetly and then Amber saw her dad out of the corner of her eye. He tapped Seth on the shoulder and asked politely if he could cut-in. Seth kissed the back of her hand and stepped away to allow her to dance with Daddy.

"How did I know he was going to do that?" her dad said after she stepped into his arms.

"Do what?"

He turned her to the side and pointed to Seth. He had stepped over to ask her mom to dance. "He plans a night like this, and now he's stealing my other girl too?"

Amber giggled. "You shouldn't have left her alone like that."

"Oh, Jewel," he said, pulling her close to him and kissing the top of her head. "What am I going to do?"

"About what?"

"That boy stealing my girl."

She laughed. "They're just dancing, Daddy. I don't think—"

"I mean this girl," he said. "This girl named Amber who God gave to me seventeen years ago. I rocked her to sleep at night and carried her around on my shoulders, taught her to swim and ride a bike and took her for her first canoe ride, and then this boy waltzes in and romances her right out of my arms."

"Like you did with Mom, you mean?"

Her dad smiled. "Yes. I suppose so."

"You know, I came across a very interesting entry in one of Grandpa's journals a few days ago."

"Oh? What was that?"

"It was when they took their trip to Europe for their twenty-fifth wedding anniversary. You don't, by any chance, remember that, do you?"

He laughed. "Yes, I remember. Three weeks was the longest amount of time I ever had to go without seeing your mother."

"Did you know Grandpa considered keeping her there—moving to Europe with his wife and two remaining unmarried children to, and I quote, 'Keep my sweet Carol from marrying that Wilson boy. I have a feeling he's going to be proposing one of these days, and by this time next year, he'll have stolen her away from me for good.'"

Her dad laughed. "Yes, I knew that. That was the first thing he said to me when I met them at the airport. Your mom hurried off the plane to see me, and when they finally caught up with her and found us kissing in the middle of the airport terminal, your grandpa tapped me on the shoulder and said, 'I brought her back, so you'd better take care of her.'"

"And you have," she said. "For what, twenty-three years now?"

"That sounds about right."

"I guess you'll have to do what Grandpa Smith did. Trust 'that boy' to take care of your little girl."

"And trust that my girl knows what she wants, will keep her eyes on Jesus, and will always go where He leads her?"

"Yes, she'll do that. I promise."

After dinner the limo driver took them to a neighborhood famous for its display of Christmas lights, and the whole evening was magical from Amber's point of view. She tried to enjoy the moment and the special night Seth had planned, and for the most part she did. He had worked too hard on this to do otherwise, but she did keep a watchful eye on Colleen and Chris.

They seemed to be talking fine tonight, and Colleen appeared to be enjoying herself, but she wondered if something was wrong. Colleen hadn't seen Chris until they pulled up to her house in the limo, and Amber didn't know if she'd had a chance to talk to Chris on the phone since yesterday.

On the way home they dropped off Chris and Colleen at Kenny's house because that's where Chris' car was. Chris was going to be driving Colleen home, and Amber prayed for them, hoping they could talk and get anything resolved that needed to be.

Amber went up to her room to change out of her dress when they arrived at the house and then rejoined Seth downstairs. Ben had left to take Hope home, and her parents had disappeared. Apparently Seth had requested a little alone-time with her in front of the fire because that's what they did for the next hour. This was their last night together here. Tomorrow they were going to her church in the morning and then they were going to Seth's house in the afternoon along with her parents to celebrate the beginning of the New Year.

She didn't get a chance to talk to Colleen until they were back at school. They met for lunch as usual, and Amber didn't waste any time asking if she'd had a chance to talk to Chris.

"Yes, we talked," she said, appearing okay but not quite herself.

"And? Is something wrong? What did he say?"

"He's thinking of going back to China this summer with the same mission team he went with two years ago."

"How do you feel about that?"

"I'm okay with it," she said. "He was afraid to tell me, but once I knew it was that, not him being unhappy with us, I felt too relieved to be mad. And I want him to go if that's where he feels God leading him. I'll miss him, of course, but I'll be okay."

"Are you still thinking of coming to camp with me?"

"Yes. Chris said I could apply to go to China too and get on the same team with him, but I don't feel God leading me there. Not yet, at least. If Chris ends up deciding to go into missions on a long-term basis, that's the area he's most interested in. His grandparents are still in Vietnam, and he's hoping to visit them this time."

"I guess we never know where we might go. In five years we could still be here in Sandy or on the other side of the world."

Colleen laughed. "Yeah, and since I finally decided I'd prefer to remain closer to home, I'll probably end up as far away as God can take me."

Amber had a basketball game that evening, and she spent the night at her grandmother's house. The following day she knew she needed to get serious about writing her term final for her writing class. She could use the story she had written about her parents but thought she might have something else inside of her. Just what, she didn't know.

Sitting on her bed after she had all of her other homework out of the way, she set her computer on her lap and wrote the title that had been swimming around in her mind ever since having dinner with Seth and everyone on Saturday.

A Dance To Remember

Thinking about all that had happened during the last month, from the Winter Dance, to her grandfather dying, to listening to Grandma's stories, and all the special times she'd had with Seth and her family, she tried to decide whom and what this Dance to remember was supposed to be about, but she came up blank. The other girl she had started writing about didn't seem to fit, and neither did real-live people like her grandparents, or herself and Seth.

She ended up writing a poem that wasn't perfect in rhyme or rhythm, and she didn't think she would use it for her assignment, but it came from her heart. Something between herself and God and the unpredictable dance called life.

I walk this path, you're by my side
I hold your hand, you hold mine
I whisper to you, 'I don't know the way'
'Just walk and believe' is all you say

Believe that I love you
Believe that I'm here
And when we're together
You have nothing to fear

I hear strange sounds, voices all around
It's all so much, they drown you out
I whisper to you, 'Are you still here?'
Yes, wait and see, I'm always near

Believe I have a plan
Believe I know the way
Just go where I go
It will be okay

I let you lead, I follow close behind
And soon I'm climbing, but I feel blind
I come through the clouds, the sun shines bright
And I say to you, 'Oh, my God, you're right!'

I have nothing to fear
You love me, You're here
Your plans were uncertain
But now they are clear

So I'll walk, run, climb, and dance
In step with you, for your truth lasts
And I'll whisper to you, 'You lead, I'll follow'
And you whisper back, 'Stay close, my daughter'

I've got big plans
Beyond your wildest dreams
Just trust me, Amber
And you will see

It's a walk worth walking,
A climb worth climbing, a dance worth dancing,

A dance to remember all that I am
Your God, your guide, your trusty friend

Your God who loves you
Your God who is here
Your God who whispers
'You have nothing to fear'

Chapter Fifteen

"He calls his own sheep by name and leads them out. When he has brought out all his own, he goes on ahead of them, and his sheep follow him because they know his voice." John 10:3-4

After Amber had written the verse for her daily Bible-reading in her journal, she immediately thought of the poem she had written the day before, and she felt a chill pass through her. One of the things that had happened during the last year, without her realizing it until this moment, was she had learned to recognize the voice of God, most of the time with unmistakable clarity: when she read the Bible, as she went about her daily life, and when she had major decisions to make.

She didn't have time to think about it right now. Stacey would be here to pick her up for school in a few minutes, but she took her journal along, knowing she would have her study period to ponder Christ's words and also on the bus this afternoon for their away basketball game at St. Mary's. The school was located in Portland, and Seth would be there to watch.

Before leaving her room, she also picked up the book sitting on her desk that Seth had given to her for Christmas. She hadn't had time to look at it yet. Actually she had, but she had been avoiding doing so. She wasn't sure why. Maybe because she thought she would discover writing a novel was way too complicated and she would never be able to do it. Or maybe because the idea simply scared her. Who was she to think she could do such a thing?

You're My daughter, Amber. And I have plans for you.

Amber put the book into her bag and headed downstairs. She grabbed a banana and a granola bar from the kitchen and went out on the front steps to wait for Stacey. It was late that evening before she returned. And she'd had a very full day.

Entering the house, she went straight to her room. She was so mad she could scream. Besides the fact she didn't say anything to her mom and dad upon her arrival, slamming her door probably hadn't been a great idea. She would rather be left alone.

"Ammie, are you okay?" her mom asked a minute later from behind the closed door.

She didn't respond.

Her mom entered the room and came to sit beside her on the bed. She had flopped onto her stomach with her face buried in her pillow. She didn't want to talk about it. She didn't want to face another day. What did it all matter if it came down to this?

"Ammie?" her mom tried again, pushing her hair to the side and gently rubbing her back. "Did something happen with Seth?"

The pillow muffled her answer. "He wasn't there."

"Do you know why?"

Not wanting her mom to think this had anything to do with him, she turned her head to the side, brushed back her tears, and answered. "He had to work late. He called me this afternoon."

"Is that what those tears are for?"

"No."

Her mom waited.

"It's Stacey," she said.

Her mom got a tissue from her desk and handed it to her.

"What's going on?" her mom asked gently. "Did you have a fight?"

Amber sat up and blew her nose, wishing it was that simple: a petty fight like they used to have in elementary school every other week.

"She's been lying to me, Mom. And I have no idea what to do."

"Lying to you? About what?"

"Her and Kenny. They've been having sex this whole time, since our sophomore year."

"She told you that?"

"No."

"Then how do you know?"

"One of her friends told me."

"How does she know?"

"Stacey told her."

"Ammie. You can't trust secondhand information. Ever. I don't care who this person is, don't believe it unless you hear it from Stacey herself."

Amber knew her mom was right, but that meant she was going to have to confront Stacey about what Paige had said to her this afternoon. She didn't know which was worse, accusing Stacey of something she hadn't done, or leaving it alone and not knowing the truth.

"What am I supposed to do?" she asked, breaking into tears again.

Her mom put her arms around her and drew her close. "First you pray and then you talk to Stacey."

"But what if it's true?"

"Then you'll keep loving her like always."

"And what if it's not and she hates me for even thinking she would lie to me?"

"If someone's saying something behind her back that's not true, I think she'll want to know that, and I think she would rather hear it from you than someone else."

Amber wished she could talk to Seth, but she knew it was too late to call. He would tell her the same thing, and she knew her mom was right, but he always encouraged her like no one else. In a way she had been relieved when she found out he wasn't coming to her game because he would know something was wrong, but she wouldn't have been able to talk about it there. But one of his supportive hugs would have been nice. Ever since she had heard Paige speak the words with such certainty this afternoon, her world had completely stopped.

"I have some good news," her mom said. "Would you like to hear it?"

"Sure."

"I didn't want to say anything to you about this until I knew for sure because I didn't want you getting your hopes up, but it's official now."

"What?"

"Uncle Tom and Aunt Beth are moving to Sandy. Tom got a job at Cedar Ridge, and they're going to move in with Grandma so she doesn't have to be alone."

Amber felt her eyes double in size. "Mandy? She's moving here too?"

Her mom smiled.

Amber squealed and fell into her mom's arms. Her concerns for Stacey fled momentarily. Leave it to God to do this today of all days!

Her mom held her tight. "I've been praying so hard. I hate thinking of Grandma being alone in that house, and I knew you would love having Mandy here."

"How soon?"

"About two weeks. Uncle Tom starts at the school at the beginning of the new semester."

"Do you think Mandy's okay with it? I mean, this is her senior year too. I'm not sure I'd want to transfer to a new school and leave all my friends behind."

"I talked to Mandy. She's actually the one who called to tell us, and she was disappointed you weren't here to tell you herself. She's thrilled, Ammie. It was her idea."

"It was?"

"Yes. She hated thinking of Grandma being alone too, and she got closer to you in a few days than she is with friends she's had for years."

"Me too. Other than Seth, I've never connected with anyone so fast."

Her mom smiled again, but Amber sensed it was for a different reason than the happy news she had shared.

"You know what your dad said when he heard you slam the door?"

"What?"

Her mom laughed and could barely get the words out. Amber started laughing too, even before she heard them.

"He said, 'Uh-oh. For once in his life, Seth must have done the wrong thing.' And I said, 'We don't know that.' And your dad said, 'I can always hope my little girl didn't find someone even more perfect than me.'"

Amber laughed. "Poor Daddy. He's not getting to use all those lectures on my boyfriend he's been writing in his head all these years."

Her mom smiled. "I think he's fine with that. I'll go break the bad news to him." Her mom glanced at her watch. "It's not that late. You should call Seth if you think he's still up. Even if you told him it was okay he couldn't be there, something tells me he's feeling bad about it anyway."

Amber didn't hesitate to reach for the phone, but as her mom opened the door, they both heard the phone ring downstairs. Her mom turned back and smiled.

"Mmmm, I wonder whom that could be?"

Amber clicked her phone on and started to say hello to Seth, but she heard her dad's voice first. She decided to stay quiet and see how this conversation went.

"Hello, Mr. Wilson," Seth said. "Is Amber home yet?"

"Yes."

There was a slight pause and then Seth said, "Could I talk to her, or is this too late to call?"

"Could I ask you something first?"

"Sure."

"Do you know why my daughter was so upset when she came home?"

Amber held in a giggle. Her dad sounded more serious with Seth than she had ever heard him. She heard the nervousness in Seth's voice when he replied.

"I wasn't able to be at her game. I had to work late. I um—she sounded all right when I talked to her though."

Amber broke in and put Seth out of his misery. "It's okay, Daddy. I'm not mad at Seth."

"Oh?"

"Sorry. He's still perfect."

Her dad laughed. "Your mom told you?"

"Yes. Could I talk to my boyfriend now?"

"Okay," he said, sounding defeated. "Sorry about that, Seth."

"Not a problem, Sir. Good night."

"Good night."

Amber busted up laughing after she heard her dad hang up. Seth laughed mildly but then asked her seriously if she was okay.

She told him the whole story. He listened and didn't hesitate to give his opinion when she finished.

"I don't think Stacey's been lying to you, sweetheart."

"I don't think so either," she said. "But why would Paige say that? She sounded like she knew what she was talking about."

"Probably because she honestly thinks they are. They've been dating for over two years, and if they hadn't started following God when they did, they probably would be."

"But you don't think they are?"

"I have a difficult time believing Stacey hasn't been honest with you. I don't think she could stand being around you, let alone be one of your best friends."

"Do you think I should let it go and not say anything?"

"I think you should do whatever you think you should do."

"Oh, thanks," she laughed. "That's helpful."

"What do you think you should do?"

"I think I should talk to her, but I don't want to," she whined.

"Believe in your friendship, Amber. If it's lasted this long, I doubt this will come between you. She knows you care about her."

"I know. Pray for me, okay?"

"I will."

"Why are you calling me?"

"To make sure you're okay. I'm sorry I wasn't there. I wouldn't have stayed, but Mr. Davidson took last week off too, so he's been swamped this week. Since he gave me all of

Winter Break off, I figured it's the least I could do. I'm working Saturday morning too. Is that okay?"

"Yeah, that's fine. Oh, guess what?"

"What?"

"Do you remember my cousin Mandy?"

"Yes."

"She's moving here in two weeks."

"To Sandy?"

"Yes! They're going to be living with Grandma. Isn't that cool?"

"That's very cool."

They talked for a little while longer about why she was happy to have her cousin moving here and her hopes that Mandy could go to Lifegate too, but she had homework to finish and so did he.

"Thanks for calling. You can turn a really bad day into a good one."

"I'm glad. I'll see you Saturday, okay?"

"Okay."

"Good night, sweetheart."

"Good night. Love you."

"I love you too, Amber. Sweet dreams."

Chapter Sixteen

On Friday morning Amber got up early enough to have a good prayer time before beginning the day. She usually had time to read her Bible, write out some initial thoughts and pray for a few minutes, but her time with God had been more rushed lately than she knew it should be, and she couldn't afford to do that today.

Opening her journal and her Bible after she got out of bed, she realized she had never written anything about the verses she read yesterday, so she read them again and wrote what was in her heart.

> *Please give me wisdom to know what, if anything, I should say to Stacey today. Help me to hear your voice clearly, and give me the courage to follow however you lead me. Give me gentle words to speak and a forgiving heart if I discover Stacey has been lying to me for the past year and a half. And give her a forgiving heart if she isn't lying and can't believe I would think otherwise.*

It was her day to drive. After she picked up Stacey, she decided to tell her on the way to school about what Paige had said and get it over with. Paige was a girl they played softball with who had become really good friends with Stacey when they had started at Sandy High their freshman year. Amber

147

had never liked her much, although she had been working on that this semester because she and Paige had *Creative Writing* together. They had worked on a joint paper back in October, and she talked to her once in awhile. But Paige had always been popular, so it wasn't like she was looking for Amber Wilson to be her friend.

The only reason she had talked to her yesterday and heard from her that Stacey and Kenny had been together—many times apparently—was because Mrs. Evans had given them class time to work on their final paper that was due next Friday. Colleen asked if she could go to her dad's classroom and use his computer because she had already started working on something, and Mrs. Evans had let her.

Amber had her free period after that, and instead of walking with Colleen toward her class like she usually did, she had walked alone and then stopped to use the bathroom. Paige was there, and while they were both washing their hands, Paige asked her how she was doing and then said something about Stacey being bummed that Kenny was going back to school on Sunday.

"I think they should go somewhere this weekend, don't you? Someplace romantic and private. If it was me, I would."

Amber felt confused by her words. "What do you mean?"

"Like the beach or up at the mountain. I told her I'd cover for her—tell her parents she's spending the night at my house. But if it was me, I'd just tell my mom where we were going and go. Her parents have to know they're having sex by now. They can't be that stupid."

Paige had started to turn away, but Amber blurted out the words she knew to be true before she could stop herself. Paige turned back and laughed.

"Oh, Amber. You're so naive it's almost sweet," she said and then left her standing there.

Amber relayed the conversation word-for-word to Stacey and then waited for her friend to respond. Stacey didn't deny that she and Paige had talked about the possibility of her and Kenny going away together this weekend, and the look on Stacey's face made her heart sink. If it wasn't true, she knew Stacey would have just denied it. She never had trouble speaking her mind when she was adamant about something. She only gave her that look when she had something she didn't want to tell her.

"Why would she say something like that, Stace?" she asked anyway, hoping with her entire being she was right and Paige was wrong.

Stacey didn't respond. Amber's heart broke. *It's true?* After talking with Seth and her mom last night she had decided it couldn't be, but everything about Stacey's unusually quiet and evasive expression told her otherwise.

"Amber, I'm not like you," she finally said. "I try to be, but you're so much stronger than me. Sometimes I feel like giving up altogether."

Amber tried to keep her emotions under control, but this was simply unbelievable. She knew she was naive about a lot of things, but she thought she knew her friends better than this.

"You've been lying to me? This whole time? Stacey!"

"Amber, calm down," Stacey said. "You can't talk and drive at the same time. Pull over."

She obeyed. They were getting close to town, and she turned onto a side-street off the highway and stopped the van along the shoulder. She started crying and Stacey leaned over and gave her a hug.

"It's okay, Amber. Calm down. Let me explain."

Explain? What's there to explain? My best friend has been lying to me about something this serious? Something I pray about constantly? Something I can't believe even now that I've heard it from Stacey herself? This is not okay!

"Kenny and I aren't having sex," Stacey said softly. "I would never lie to you about that."

"But you said—"

Stacey sat back and faced her. "No, Amber. You misunderstood what I said. I haven't been lying to you. I've been lying to Paige."

Amber stared at her, not sure what she meant. Stacey explained herself.

"Back when Kenny and I were first dating, me and Paige were really good friends, and she kept asking me about when I was going to have sex with him, and I felt too stupid to tell her I didn't feel ready for that, so I finally told her we did and let her continue to assume we have been ever since.

"That's one of the reasons I was thinking of breaking up with Kenny that summer. I knew he was fine with us waiting, but I didn't know how long that would last, and I felt so much pressure from Paige and my other friends to not be a virgin, that I didn't know how much longer I could keep lying to them without Kenny finding out or just going ahead and doing it.

"I'll never forget that night Loralyn talked to us at camp about how she was waiting. It was such a relief to know I wasn't the only one who had been dating a guy for a year and hadn't had sex with him yet. And she was even older than me. For the first time in six months I didn't feel like a total freak, you know?"

Amber nodded. "I know. I understand, Stacey."

"I know you're great about being honest with people and letting them know you're waiting, but I still have a hard time with that, especially with girls like Paige who I've already lied to. It's easier to keep letting her assume. I know I shouldn't. I should tell her the truth, but it's not the easiest thing to blurt out. I almost told her when she was trying to get me to set up something special for Kenny this weekend, but it's easier for me to hide behind my parents and say, 'I'd get caught, I know it' than to say, 'I lied to you, Paige. Kenny and I have never had sex, and we're waiting until we get married.'"

Amber gave her a hug. "It's okay, Stace. You don't need to tell her anything if you don't want to. What's important is what's going on between you and Kenny. That's what I care about."

"I know, Amber. You want to know something funny?"

She knew they needed to get going, but she waited for Stacey to finish. "Of all my friends back then, you were the first one I told the truth to, but I wasn't sure you believed me."

"Of course I believed you," she said. "I was too naive to not believe you."

They both laughed. Once they were back on the highway, Stacey said she did think she needed to set the record straight with Paige and knew this was the perfect opportunity to do so.

"Are you mad I doubted you, Stace?"

"No. You had every right to after what Paige said, and I'm glad you told me because now I can to go to her and say, 'You can call me a liar and hate my guts, but don't you dare tell my best friend she's so naive it's almost sweet."

"You don't have to defend me, Stace. And you can have much more of a positive influence on someone like Paige than I ever could. God has a way of taking our mistakes and using them for good. Give Him a chance to do that, okay?"

"Amber Wilson, you are the most optimistic and fearless person I know."

"I don't think so. You have no idea how much I was shaking on the way to pick you up this morning."

"Fear isn't about what you feel; it's about what you do. And you've always had the courage to speak your mind with me."

"Jesus gives me courage, Stace. And He will give it to you too."

***

That evening Amber didn't have any trouble writing another short story. She kept the title she had thought of before, *A Dance To Remember,* and wrote about a girl like Stacey who had been dating a guy she really liked and was going to the prom with. She was also seriously considering losing her virginity that night, mostly because her friends were pressuring her to, but she ended up talking to her boyfriend instead, letting him know how she felt, and was pleasantly surprised to discover he was fine with waiting and was dating her because he really liked her too, not just to get her into bed.

She showed the story to Seth the following afternoon. He liked it and complimented her writing like always, but she hadn't shown it to him to hear his praise. God had spoken to her clearly last night after she had finished the story, and she wanted to share His words with him.

"God wants me to write fictional stories for teens that are based on the truth: the truth I've seen at work in my own life and the lives of my family members and friends."

"Does that mean you're going to be writing about you and me?"

"I think so. I'll change some of the circumstances, and the characters will be like me and you and my friends in some ways, and different in others, but the truth of God's perfect ways and how He works will be the same, based on what I've seen Him do in my own real life."

"That's very cool," Seth said, stopping her in the middle of the bridge at Wildwood and giving her a kiss. "You certainly know how to write a good kissing scene."

She knew he was referring to the one she had included in her story. Her "Kenny" character had kissed "Stacey" several times that evening, but the best one came at the end of the night when they shared a very love-filled kiss based on their mutual agreement that their relationship went beyond fleeting moments of pleasure and things they weren't ready for.

She planned to use the short story for her writing assignment now, but she also wanted to go back and start writing about these characters from the time they first met, through the night of the dance, to the way they end up both finding Jesus, falling completely in love with each other, and doing whatever God leads them to do.

She had spent all morning reading the book Seth had given her and was beginning to see how she could make it all come together with good character development, plot-lines, and taking the time to write in a way God had gifted her to do.

"I was talking to my mom and dad about when we might be able to go visit the Lifegate campus again," Seth said, changing the subject. "They thought maybe we could go during Spring Break and make a whole week out of it. What do you think? Are you interested in going on vacation with my family to California?"

"I think I might be," she said, receiving another sweet kiss.

"Some warm California sun sounds good right now. It's freezing up here today."

"I know," she said, rubbing her cold nose on his. "You'd better hold me close or I might turn into a snow angel."

"Or a snow princess," he whispered. "Uh-oh, too late."

She smiled. "I don't think I can write about boys like you in my stories. No one will ever believe in such a sweet and romantic guy."

"Sure you can. You just have to give him some flaws too."

"Oh? Like what?"

"Like that he has no fashion sense and doesn't know how to wear his hair without his sister's help."

"Or he doesn't usually sleep-in and he's bad at water-skiing?"

"Yeah, throw in a few things like that."

"I'm still not sure anyone would believe it."

"They might not, but it doesn't change the truth."

"The truth that guys like you really do exist and a plain country girl managed to find one?"

"No, that a beautiful, Jesus-loving, equally unbelievable girl stole his heart with her sweet smile, spilled Pepsi, and her heart-stopping kisses."

He kissed her gently and added, "You're my dream-girl, Amber, but you're one-hundred percent real. And don't think for a second that still doesn't blow my mind, baby."

Dear Reader,

Fact or fiction? What do you think? Are these stories about Amber and Seth too good to be true? Do guys like Seth really exist? Does God bless those who seek Him? Amber and Seth are characters from my imagination, but their seeking hearts, actions, attitudes, and the way God guides them is based on truth: the truth God teaches us in the Bible and the ways I have seen Him work.

My husband and I have been involved in ministry for many years, starting when we were teenagers working at a youth camp similar to the one where Amber and Seth meet. And I've met many girls like Amber, Stacey, Nicole, and Colleen. And I've known guys like Seth (I married one), and I've also known those like Kenny, Spencer, and Matt. No two people are exactly alike. No two circumstances are either. But God's ways do not change. Jesus is the same yesterday, today, and forever. That means the ways I have seen Him work in my life can be true for you too.

No matter who you are, what your life is like, what mistakes you've made, or how insignificant or inadequate you feel, putting your life in the hands of Jesus and living the way He says is best can make a real difference in your life. God wants to bless you. He wants you to experience His love. He wants you to be whole, to be filled with joy and peace, to feel loved and have a loving heart like His. Give your heart and life completely over to Jesus, and then wait and see what He does. In other words:

Trust in the LORD with all your heart, and do not lean on your own understanding. In all your ways acknowledge him, and he will make your paths straight.
(Proverbs 3:5-6)

*I'd love to hear how God has used
this story to touch your heart.*

Write me at:

living_loved@yahoo.com

.

Printed in Great Britain
by Amazon

25039531R00089